DEA

Dead Man's Chest is th_____
series. The other titles _____
Wake Up, It's Midnight _____
Locked Doors and *Ghost* _____

NAITABAL:	A wild species of human, aged about ten.
NAITABAL LANGUAGE:	Language used by Naitabals to confuse enemies and adults.
NAITABAL OAK:	An oak tree suitable for habitation by Naitabals.
NAITABAL TERRITORY:	Any land occupied or controlled by Naitabals.
NAITAGONIA:	Any foreign soil in England occupied by Naitabals.

David Schutte was born in Crouch End, North London. Brain surgeon, pop singer and Olympic athlete are just some of the things he never achieved. Apart from being an author, he is also a specialist children's bookseller. He lives in Hampshire with his wife and children.

Also by David Schutte

SAM and the U.F.O.

The Naitabal Mystery series:

1. DANGER, KEEP OUT!
   (Originally published as MUD PIES AND WATER-BOMBS)

2. WAKE UP, IT'S MIDNIGHT!

3. WILD WOODS, DARK SECRET

4. BEHIND LOCKED DOORS

SKELETONS IN THE ATTIC   (A non-Naitabal *prequel*
                               to GHOST ISLAND)

5. GHOST ISLAND

6. DEAD MAN'S CHEST

Non-fiction:

WILLIAM – THE IMMORTAL An illustrated Bibliography

DAVID SCHUTTE

DEAD MAN'S CHEST

A Naitabal Mystery

To Liam

David Schutte

Junior Genius

First published in 2001 by Junior Genius
93 Milford Hill, Salisbury, Wiltshire SP1 2QL

ISBN 1-904028-06-3

1 3 5 7 9 8 6 4 2

A CIP catalogue record for this book
is available from the British Library

Printed in the U.K. by
Polestar AUP Aberdeen Ltd

TO

my brother Jim

who loves exploring

Rules for Speaking Naitabal Language

Words beginning with A: Add 'ang' to the end.
e.g. apple = *apple-ang*. The word 'a', however, is just *ang*.

Words beginning with B,C or D: move the first letter to the end of the word, then add 'ang' to the end.
e.g. banana = *anana-bang*; catapult = *atapult-cang*;
    disaster = *isaster-dang*.

Words beginning with E: Add 'eng' to the end.
e.g. elephant = *elephant-eng*.

Words beginning with F,G or H: move the first letter to the end of the word, then add 'eng' to the end.
e.g. fool = *ool-feng*; groan = *roan-geng*; help = *elp-heng*.

Words beginning with I: Add 'ing' to the end.
e.g. ink = *ink-ing*. The word 'I', however, is just *Ing*.

Words beginning with J,K,L,M, or N: move the first letter to the end of the word, then add 'ing' to the end.
e.g. jump = *ump-jing*; kill = *ill-king*; laugh = *augh-ling*;
    measles = *easles-ming*; night = *ight-ning*.

Words beginning with O: Add 'ong' to the end.
e.g. orange = *orange-ong*.

Words beginning with P,Q,R,S, or T: move the first letter to the end of the word, then add 'ong' to the end.

e.g. parrot = *arrot-pong*; queen = *een-quong* (notice that 'qu' stays together); rabbit = *abbit-rong*;
    sausage = *ausage-song*; tickle = *ickle-tong*.

Words beginning with U: Add 'ung' to the end.

e.g. under = *under-ung*.

Words beginning with V,W,X,Y or Z: Move the first letter to the end of the word, then add 'ung' to the end.

e.g. vest = *est-vung*; witch = *itch-wung*; xylophone = *ylophone-xung*; young = *oung-yung*; zebra = *ebra-zung*.

For words beginning with CH,GH,PH,RH,SH,TH, or WH, move the 'H' with the first letter, but follow the 'first letter' rules.

e.g. chop = *op-chang*; ghost = *ost-gheng*; photo = *oto-phong*;
    rhesus = *esus-rhong*; shop = *op-shong*;
    thistle = *istle-thong*; why = *y-whung*.

For plurals, keep the 's' in the original position.

e.g. book = *ook-bang*; books = *ooks-bang*;
    pig = *ig-pong*; pigs = *igs-pong*.

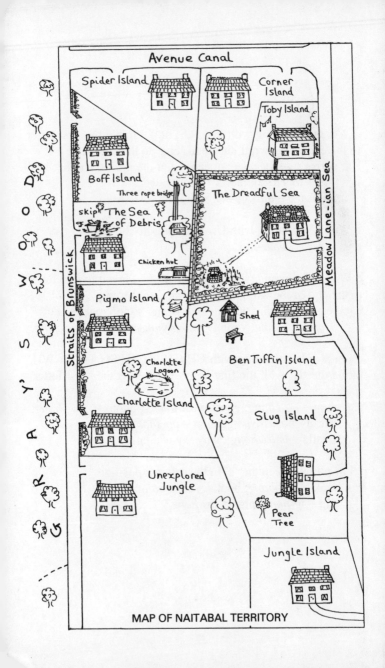

MAP OF NAITABAL TERRITORY

Contents

CHAPTER ONE

Deep Shadow Cottage

There was only one cottage in the eastern half of Gray's Wood. All year long it stood dark and silent, all alone in the thick shadows of trees that crowded its little space. Two muddy ruts ventured cautiously towards its broken wooden gate, but stopped short several metres away, as if afraid to go any closer. Strange footprints sometimes appeared when the earth was soft, but no one could be sure if they belonged to its owner, or just curious passers-by. As far as the Naitabals knew, no one lived there.

Even its name was a mystery – Deep Shadow Cottage.

Gray's Wood was an ancient wood that sprawled between Naitabal territory and the river to the west. The Naitabals often played games in its dark interior, yet for all the times they passed the cottage they had never seen signs of life inside. They never saw anyone approaching or leaving, never saw smoke climbing lazily from its chimney, and never saw a single movement at its windows.

Until today.

Today, a girl came running along the muddy track like a bullet, a ten-year-old girl with jet black hair and bright blue eyes. Her feet thumped in the soft earth, leaving their marks before she veered off at an angle along the paths she knew well, running as fast as her legs could manage. She eventually reached the road, swerved left, turned right at the end and right again, and into the front garden of the first house.

It was Jayne. Jayne was a Naitabal. Her hot, breathless body hurtled up the short gravel path and collided with

Toby's front door with a mighty thump. She stabbed at the bell and assaulted the knocker and jumped up and down impatiently, waiting for someone to answer.

"Come on, Toby! Come on! Don't be asleep!"

She said the words through the letterbox over and over again like a mantra, repeating them urgently to make them come true.

"Come on, Toby! Come on! Don't be asleep!"

Five more knocks and six more rings later, the door slowly opened at last, and Toby's dishevelled form appeared in the gloom like a zombie just out of its grave.

Before Toby's eyes could focus, Jayne blurted out her message.

"I was in Gray's Wood and I saw a face at the window!"

Toby stood for a few seconds, eyes half closed, waiting for the incoming message to kick-start his brain. At last something stirred and a glimmer of intelligence shone through.

"You're trying to catch me out," he said in his solemn voice. "Woods don't have windows."

Jayne almost screamed.

"Toby! Wake up! I'm talking about the *cottage* in Gray's Wood! Deep Shadow Cottage! I saw a face at the window!"

That was enough. Suddenly, Toby was awake.

"You're joking! When? What did you see?"

"Get dressed and come and look!" said Jayne. "Before he's gone! Come on!"

Toby disappeared into the house and emerged two minutes later in jeans and a thick jumper. He hadn't bothered with shoes or socks – Toby often went barefoot, anyway. He and Jayne set off at a trot northwards to the top of the Meadowlane-ian Sea (it was Meadow Lane to ordinary people). They ran west along Avenue Canal, then headed south on to the Straits of Brunswick until they reached the first entrance to Gray's Wood on the right.

"What about the others?" said Toby, meaning the other three Naitabals. "Shouldn't we tell them as well?"

Jayne didn't stop running but led him further into the wood as she explained.

"There's no time," she panted. "Anyway, Ben's out with his mum and dad, Boff's out with *his* mum and dad, and Charlotte's out with *her* mum and dad. Saturday morning shopping. I came into Gray's Wood to look at the green woodpecker's nest. I didn't bother calling for you. I knew you'd still be sleep."

"You were right."

"I know."

"What time is it, then? I forgot to grab my watch."

Jayne looked at her own.

"Eight-thirty," she said.

"Eight-thirty! That's like the small hours of the morning! I never get up till eleven on a Saturday."

"You do when there's something exciting happening," said Jayne, "and there's something exciting happening now."

"That's different, then."

They had penetrated deep into the woods by this time, and Jayne raised a finger to her lips.

"We'd better keep quiet," she said, "in case anyone hears us."

As they approached the cottage, the shadows crowded in on them. Jayne led Toby to a mass of undergrowth where they could watch without being seen.

"Is this where you were?" Toby hissed, his bare feet not seeming to mind the rough ground.

"Yes. I saw the face at that window on the left, the one downstairs."

They crouched for half an hour in almost complete silence, waiting for something else to happen in the cottage. But nothing did. No hand moved its raggy curtains, and no face appeared at its windows again. The only shadows that moved across its walls were the crooked shapes of twigs and branches as they lurched in the gusty breeze that whipped through the wood.

"You must have imagined it," said Toby.

"I didn't!" said Jayne, offended. "I saw a face. A real face."

"Was it a man or a woman?"

"I don't know. I was too far away. It might have been a child for all I know."

"I don't think a child would live there on its own," said Toby.

"No, but it would be exciting if one did, wouldn't it?" Jayne grinned. "I'd love to have a house in the woods, wouldn't you? With no one around for miles."

"No I wouldn't. Not with all those leaves to rake up every autumn."

Jayne laughed.

"And people murdering me every day," Toby added.

"They wouldn't murder you *every* day," said Jayne, turning a sinister look on him. "Once is usually enough."

Soon afterwards they emerged from their spying-place and moved closer to the cottage. There was no vehicle parked on the rough track that led to its gate on the far side, and there were no tyre tracks or footprints in the mud.

They stayed for another half an hour, then hurried back to see if the other Naitabals were home, and to tell them the news.

Over the days that followed, all five Naitabals took it in turns to watch the cottage in case the face appeared again. But none of them saw anything.

None of them could have guessed at the secrets the cottage was hiding. None of them would have believed that a child's lost teddy bear would help them to solve its mystery. After all, if it hadn't been for the teddy bear, the secret might never have come to light. . . And, of course, if it hadn't been for

14

the rubbish sack, the teddy bear might never have been found. . . And if it hadn't been for the Naitabals – and the dead man's chest – even Gray's Wood itself might have been lost forever. . .

It was a whole week since Jayne had seen the face at the window. Three of the days had passed with no sighting at Deep Shadow Cottage. Then it had started raining – heavily. It had been raining for the past four days, which meant that further spying activities had been abandoned.

The Naitabals' headquarters was a tree-house that sat astride the branches of a huge oak tree at the bottom of Mr Elliott's garden. The garden was full of forty-years' worth of builder's rubbish and was known to the Naitabals as the Sea of Debris. It was dry and warm inside the tree-house, but today the windows were steamed up and rain-spattered, and it was impossible to see anything outside. Even if the Naitabals could have spied out of the windows, there were no humans to spy on, because no one with any sense was out of doors in such terrible weather.

They did, of course, have one neighbour without any sense, and that was Cedric Morgan, the leader of the enemy Igmopong. But even Cedric was indoors, although it wasn't because he had suddenly and miraculously become sensible. It was because Cedric and his bossy sister Doris were both bedridden, recovering from a bout of flu. Given the choice, Cedric would have preferred being huddled in his own ramshackle tree-house, pelted by rain and wind through its non-existent walls, shouting insults at the Naitabals next door. Cedric and his gang were insanely jealous of the Naitabals' magnificent upper-class tree-house, which had been built for them by Mr Elliott, the builder. Their dearest wish in life was to have it for themselves.

But even Pigmo Island (known to the rest of the world as Cedric's garden) was deserted.

15

With nothing else to do, the Naitabals were on their third game of Monopoly. To make it more interesting they allowed anyone who threw double six to make a new rule. So far, Charlotte had changed all the street names to islands, and Boff had turned the different values of banknotes into military aircraft, ships, guns and ammunition.

Now it was Ben's turn.

"Double six!" shouted Charlotte. "That means you've landed on Tristan Da Cuhna and you owe me three Exocet Missiles. And double six means you can make a new rule."

"I know," said Ben, moving his red acorn and handing over the rent. "I've thought of one already. From now on, jail is Cedric's tree-house."

"Tree-*plank*," said Toby. "You can't call it a tree-*house* when it's just planks nailed to the branches and two doors for a roof."

"Okay," said Ben. "Tree-plank. If you go to jail, you have to go out of here, cross the fence to Pigmo Island, and climb up into the Igmopong's tree-plank."

"It's pouring with rain and blowing half a hurricane," Jayne protested. "We'll get soaked."

"That's why you'll need a 'Get Out of Gale' card," said Ben, and laughed a lot.

Unfortunately, Ben laughed too much. Minutes later he was the first to go to jail. It was the others' turn to laugh as they watched Ben open the trap-door in the floor, unfurl the rope ladder and slither down in the slanting rain and wind to make his way to the tree-house on Pigmo Island. He stood shivering on its slippery, sloping floor, holding tight to a branch for safety, waiting for the others to take their turns (and his) and end his misery.

The others, of course, took their turns painfully slowly on purpose, trying to teach Ben a lesson for inventing such a mad rule. Charlotte threw open the south window and yelled a running commentary at Ben on their slow progress.

"It's Toby's turn. He's shaking the dice. He's stopped to scratch his nose. Now he's shaking the dice again. He's shaking them a lot. . . Oh! He's dropped one! Oops! He can't find it! We're all looking for it. Ah, we've got it! He's shaking them again! Oops, clumsy! He's dropped both of them this time. . ."

They all laughed a lot, and Ben sat grinning in the Igmopong tree, soaked to the skin.

At last, Charlotte shouted the good news.

"You had your turn and you threw a double!" she called. "You're free!"

Ben came back, drenched, and Charlotte gave him the bad news.

"You threw a double, but you landed on Sri Lanka. That'll cost you three Harrier jump-jets and five tanks, please."

Five minutes later, it was Jayne who picked up a Chance card and read it aloud.

"Oh, no. 'Go to Cedric's tree-plank, go directly to Cedric's tree-plank, do not pass Mr Elliott's chicken run, do not collect 200 egg grenades.' I'm in jail!"

Within half an hour they had all been to jail and they were all soaked through. They decided it was time to go to Charlotte's house to dry out and have some hot drinks.

Back in the Naitabal hut again, with no end to the rain in sight, they decided to play cards. They spent the next hour sticking labels on a pack of cards to make four *Naitabal* suits. Instead of clubs, diamonds, hearts and spades, they had shrubs, slimeponds, tarts and glades. The thirteen cards in each suit became natural disasters ranging in seriousness from two (Rain) to ace (Meteorite).

"The order," said Toby, just to remind them, "is two, Rain; three, Sleet; four, Wind; five, Hail; six, Lightning; seven, Blizzard; eight, Gale; nine, Hurricane; ten, Tornado; jack, Volcano; queen, Earthquake; king, Tidal Wave; ace, Meteorite."

17

"My Tidal Wave of Slimeponds beats your Volcano of Tarts, then," said Jayne.

Ten games later they had abandoned the cards. Ben was playing noughts and crosses in the steam of the window, Toby was catching up on some sleep, Boff was doing a crossword, and Jayne and Charlotte were practising magic tricks with coins.

"We've got to think of something else to do," Ben said suddenly, when boredom had finally driven him to speech. He was the most adventurous of the Naitabals, and he was missing the great outdoors. "We've all read everyone else's comics, we've all read each other's books, we've played everything we can think of, and I'm bored."

"Yes," agreed Charlotte. "We should be out climbing trees."

The rain was easing at last, and Jayne peered through the misted glass at Mr Elliott's rubbish-filled garden, which was just becoming visible again.

"The Sea of Debris," she announced, "is a Sea of Mud."

"We haven't even had the Igmopong to laugh at," said Toby, stirring.

"It's typical, isn't it," said Boff, taking his glasses off and cleaning them. "The moment the Igmopong are out of our way, bedridden with flu, it rains for four days."

It was true. The Igmopong always interfered with everything the Naitabals tried to do. The flu had been the Naitabals' first opportunity for months to be rid of Cedric Morgan and his irritating gang and get their teeth into something exciting. But the rain had had different ideas.

They needn't have worried, though, because adventure was not far away. It had stopped raining at last, and Deep Shadow Cottage was calling.

18

Cedric's Secret

Cedric Morgan and his sister Doris had been taken ill a week ago and had been in bed ever since. Doris's bed had been moved into Cedric's room so that they could keep each other company.

Mrs Morgan was large and highly emotional, and had decided from Day One that both her children were at death's door. She had refused to listen to the opinions of three different doctors (who had been called out in the small hours of three consecutive nights), and ignored the fact that twenty other local children had had the same symptoms and had recovered rapidly to perfect (rude and noisy) health. But Mrs Morgan wailed and moaned and bullied the doctors.

When it was completely obvious to everyone but a brain-dead carrot that her precious darlings were going to live, she was so relieved that she nearly killed them both by hugging them to death. In her ecstasy she promised them a special treat. In fact, anything they wanted. Cedric and Doris had always been spoilt, but to make them a promise like this was not a good idea.

During their livelier moments of illness, Cedric and Doris had been reading stories to each other. It so happened that practically every story featured a midnight feast. As they had both been deprived of food for almost a week (a great shock to their normally well-nourished systems), their choice of reward was really rather predictable.

Even as the Naitabals were shinning down the rope ladder from the Naitabal tree-house, so Cedric was voicing their decision. Unfortunately, he still had a blocked-up nose, and the words didn't come out very clearly.

"We wadt a bid-dight feast," he announced.

"Of course you can have a midnight feast, darlings," said Mrs Morgan. She gave each of them another life-threatening hug against her airtight bosom, releasing them shortly before the first signs of death. "I think it's a lovely idea."

Unfortunately, Mrs Morgan did not really understand the essential secret nature of midnight feasts, and spoilt it by adding, "You can have it in one of your bedrooms with all your friends."

Cedric and Doris's faces dropped, and their sore throats and blocked noses grumbled incomprehensible words of protest.

"But, Bub—"

"Dot id our *bed*roobs—"

What they were trying to say was that midnight feasts in bedrooms – if parents knew about them – lacked the flavour of lawlessness that was necessary for midnight feasts. It had to be somewhere exciting. In the last adventure story they'd read, the midnight feast had been at the bottom of a disused mine-shaft.

"We wadt it at the bottob ob a bide-shaft."

"At the what?" said Mrs Morgan. "What's a bide-shaft?"

"No, a *bide*-shaft!"

"That's what I said, dear. Anyway, whatever it is, we haven't got one. You'll have to think of something sensible. Something *safe*."

Mrs Morgan left them together to discuss it.

"It could be id the tedt," said Doris.

Cedric paused while he tried to work out what a 'tedt' was.

"Oh, you bead a *tedt*," he said, and only then realised that with his blocked nose he couldn't say "tent" either. "We've had huddreds of bid-dight feasts id the tedt," he added, scoffing. "We've eved had wud of the silly old Daitabals' bid-dight feasts id the tedt."

"What about the tree-house, thed?"

"We've had *billiods* of bid-dight feasts id *there*."

"Well, you thig of subwhere."

Cedric tried to blow his nose clear, but without success.

"You'll blow your braids out if you're dot careful," said Doris. "Add you haved't got buch left eddyway."

This insult spurred Cedric on to think of somewhere really exotic. In a sudden triumph of inspiration he thought of Gray's Wood.

Doris approved and they called for their mother.

"Bub! Bub!"

Mrs Morgan rushed back. She listened patiently to their suggestion, and was horrified.

"But Cedric, darling, Doris, sweetie, you can't have a midnight feast in the *woods*. I worry enough when you're all out in that flimsy tent in the garden. The most dreadful things could happen. . ."

Cedric and Doris's faces, already pale from the flu, went even paler as their mother told them some of the dreadful things that might happen in a wood at midnight.

"You could be *ripped apart* by a bear," she said.

Cedric tried to gulp, but failed.

"Dere ared't ady bears in dis coudtry," he protested.

"They escape from zoos, sweetheart," snapped Mrs Morgan. "So do lions, tigers, panthers and leopards. You wouldn't want to be *ripped apart* by one of those, would you? They like *ten and eleven-year-old* children best of all, because there's plenty of fresh young meat on them."

"Dey always say if adibals escape," said Doris, shivering. "Hab dey said anythigg, ded?"

"No, dear, but it'll be too late if you're in the woods having a midnight feast and it comes up on the television that a pack of wolves has escaped. It's even worse being eaten by wolves," Mrs Morgan went on. "One of them sinks its teeth into your head, four more get your legs and arms,

21

and they pull in five different directions."

Cedric and Doris closed their legs.

"We dod't mide," said Doris. "We'll tayg a chadce."

"The only bit they leave is your scalp. They don't like hair."

"Dat's okay," said Cedric.

"There are worse things than wild animals," Mrs Morgan went on heartlessly.

"Wadt?"

"Nasty people," said Mrs Morgan darkly. "People who sell *boy-meat* to the shops to make pork pies. Well, they *call* them pork pies. . ."

"Wadt about girl-beat?" said Cedric, looking across at Doris.

"Same thing," said Mrs Morgan. "But girls taste more like chicken."

For a moment – but only for one moment – Cedric and Doris wavered. But then their dream of the feast took a firm hold again. They insisted that it must take place in the woods, and they were adamant that it should take place at midnight. They reminded their mother that she had promised them anything they wanted. Nothing else would do.

Then Mrs Morgan had another daft idea.

"Of course it'll be all right," she said brightly. "Mummy was only joking! Daddy and the other fathers will be there with you to keep you all safe."

Cedric and Doris were so disgusted with this suggestion that they promptly had relapses and started feigning imminent death.

"Oh, darlings, darlings, don't do that!" cried Mrs Morgan. She tried to hug both their limp bodies at once. She was used to their tantrums, but this was the sort she hated most. "Mummy understands, she really does!"

Cedric's eyelids fluttered closed as he tried to look as near to death as possible. No air could get in or out of his nose, so he hung his mouth open and made gurgling noises instead. On Mrs Morgan's other arm, Doris was doing the same thing. Simultaneously, after a spasm signal from Cedric, they both stopped breathing. They had done it scores of times before, and it always gave their mother something close to a heart attack.

"All right, darlings! All right! Don't do it – you're frightening Mummy!"

Cedric's eyes fluttered open again. Mrs Morgan put her ear to his mouth to listen to the weak, pathetic whisper that came out.

"We dode wodd eddy-wud dere," it said.

"Of course not, darlings, of course not! Mummy was only joking again!" She clutched her son's fast-fading form to her chest. "Of course you can have your feast with no one there!"

Seconds after this promise, Cedric and Doris made miraculous recoveries and sat up. Mrs Morgan, overjoyed at the miracle, hugged them senseless again and added, "But there'll have to be *some* sort of supervision."

The thought of *some* supervision made Doris and Cedric wish they had dragged out their dying moments a little longer. But then another thought struck Cedric and he was suddenly filled with alarm.

"Add we dod't wadt the Daitabals to fide out, eidder," he warned.

He knew only too well that if the Naitabals heard what was being planned, disaster was sure to follow. He had played so many tricks on them in the past, they were sure to grab at any chance to get their own back. He made his mother promise that everyone involved would be sworn to the utmost secrecy.

The Naitabals were dying to know if there had been any

23

developments at Deep Shadow Cottage, and Jayne and Toby were the first to go looking. There was no sign of movement as they approached. They found a clump of overgrown brambles and watched from behind it for ten minutes before moving closer.

"There's no one there," said Jayne. "I've been wondering for days if I really saw anyone. But I know I did."

"Let's go and have a proper look in the window," said Toby.

"We can't," said Jayne. "We'd have to go into the garden to look in the windows."

"That's why no one ever looks in there. We can always say we saw someone at the window, and we thought they might be in trouble."

"Okay," said Jayne, who didn't need much convincing. "Come on, then."

They approached the cottage together. Its little square of ground was surrounded by a low stone wall which was topped with a wooden trellis. The trellis was falling to pieces, overgrown with ivy and honeysuckle that were probably the only things keeping it upright.

They made their way cautiously to the only entrance, a single wooden gate that faced the rough rutted track. The track meandered out through the trees for a quarter of a mile to a five-bar gate by the road. Toby raised the latch and they walked into the little yard that led to the front door. From here it was possible to walk right round the cottage in either direction.

"Let's knock first," said Jayne, suddenly worried. She dropped her voice to a whisper. "We can ask for a drink of water if anyone answers."

Toby nodded and Jayne raised the big knocker and dropped it hard against the door. The big hollow sound echoed eerily through the little house and reverberated in the trees all around them. A few rooks flapped in the canopy, swearing, then the silence that followed seemed even deeper than before Jayne had knocked.

"It sounds really spooky," whispered Toby. "Better try again."

Jayne repeated the summons, twice in quick succession, but there was no answer other than the curses of the rooks. Satisfied that there was no one at home, she and Toby turned to the left and crept along, pausing at each window to look inside. It was gloomy enough in the woods, but even darker in the cottage. All they could see through the windows were ornaments and shadows of furniture, but no signs of life or recent habitation. It was when they had come almost full circle that they were literally stopped in their tracks.

"Oh, look!" said Jayne. "The foxes have been at the rubbish."

It was true. A big black dustbin bag of rubbish, knotted at the top, had been chewed open at the side. The contents were strewn across the space between the surrounding wall and the cottage. There were tin cans, cardboard packets, paper and banana skins and just about everything found in most people's rubbish bins.

Toby poked some of it with his foot, then picked up a flattened milk carton and read the top. "Hey, look!" he said, showing Jayne. "You know what this means?"

"Yes," said Jayne. "Milk. But foxes can't read."

Toby grinned. "No! Look at the sell-by date. It means someone's been here recently, doesn't it?"

Jayne looked at the carton and then at Toby with widening eyes.

"Toby, yes!" she said excitedly. "Of course it does! I wasn't going mad after all! I *knew* I'd seen someone!"

"We'd better clear it up," said Toby. "Come on."

They both set to work pushing the debris back into the hole in the side of the sack. They were half finished when something else caught Toby's eye. He stooped down to take

25

a closer look, and slid out half a sheet of paper from under a pile of orange peel.

"What's that?" said Jayne.

"Just something I noticed," said Toby, staring at it. "It's the plan of a room. Look." Toby straightened out the crumpled sheet and pressed it flat on the wall so they could both see it. "It's the word 'hidden' that made me pick it up," he added.

It was a sheet of blue notepaper, but most of the writing on it had been crossed out before it had been thrown away. Sure enough, the word 'hidden' was written clearly near the top, in a sentence that said, simply, 'X – TEDDY BEAR HIDDEN HERE.'

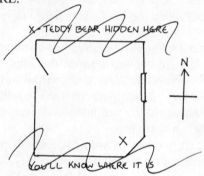

"I wonder why it's all crossed out?" said Toby.

Jayne thought about it.

"It must have been rewritten," she said. "I bet this was just a rough. I do that sometimes, don't you? There's loads of crossed-out sheets in my waste-paper bin."

They squinted at the plan.

"It looks like a room with a window and a door opposite," said Toby.

"Like half the rooms in the world, nearly," said Jayne.

"And marked with a cross in the corner."

"That's the 'X'," said Jayne. "'Teddy Bear Hidden Here.' How are we supposed to tell where it is, or which room it is?"

"We're not," said Toby. "Look near the bottom. It says 'YOU'LL KNOW WHERE IT IS.' They don't want to tell strangers where it is, do they?"

"Why would someone want to hide a teddy bear?"

"How should I know? Perhaps it's been naughty."

"Now you're being silly."

"Perhaps it's part of a hoard of teddy bears from the Great Teddy Bear Robbery. They're being sold into slavery."

Jayne giggled, then looked round. "Perhaps there's another sheet that explains more."

"I bet there isn't."

"I'm going to look anyway."

Jayne started rummaging through the rest of the rubbish. There were no envelopes addressed to anyone to give them a clue, and no other pages of writing at all. It began to get smelly and unpleasant, so they eventually pushed everything into the black bin liner and sealed up the ragged hole as best they could.

"That's a pity," said Jayne.

"It must be one of the rooms here," said Toby at last. "In Deep Shadow Cottage."

"I bet you're right. Come on, let's go and tell the others what we've found. They'll be excited when we show them this!"

It was just beginning to drizzle again as they left the narrow little garden. They went out through the gate, taking care to close it behind them, then made their way through the woods and across the road back home to Naitabal territory.

Back in the Naitabal hut, the five Naitabals were discussing what Toby and Jayne had found.

"It's just a diagram of a room," said Boff, holding it on the floor where everyone could see it.

"And in the corner of the room, there – " said Jayne, pointing, "is the cross." She moved her finger to the top of the sheet. "And there. . . it shows the cross again."

"Teddy Bear Hidden Here," murmured Charlotte. "It's really strange, isn't it?"

"You can say that again," said Ben.

"The trouble is," said Toby, "we don't know if it means a room in the cottage or not. It was too dark to see much inside. Anyway, what was there to see?"

"Look," said Boff. "This compass point shows that the window in the diagram faces east. Do any of the cottage windows face east?"

They all thought about it.

"No," said Charlotte at last. "There's one blank wall on the cottage, the one at the opposite end to the gate. I bet that's about east, when you think about it."

"That means it can't be a room at the cottage, then," said Boff.

"Well, if it isn't a room in the cottage," said Ben, "we don't stand a chance. It could be a house anywhere in the country."

"Or the world," said Toby.

"The only strange thing about the room," said Boff, "is this bit." He stabbed a finger at the south-eastern corner near the 'X'. "Have you ever seen a room with the corner cut off like that?"

No one had.

"Every room I've ever been in has got square corners," said Charlotte.

"And me," said Jayne.

"And me," said Ben and Toby together.

"I know!" said Charlotte.

"What?" said Ben.

"Let's ask Mr Elliott!"

It was obvious now that Charlotte had said it. Mr Elliott had been a builder for forty years and had worked on practically every house for miles around. He worked all the hours of daylight, and half the hours of night, and only came home to eat and sleep.

"Hey, it's lunch-time!" shouted Ben. "He might be home!"

They were lucky. Minutes later they were standing in Mr Elliott's kitchen, where their best friend was tucking into an enormous pile of bacon, eggs, tomatoes and fried bread, and sipping tea from a gigantic mug with 'EDDIE' on the side.

"Help yerselves to anythin' you want," he said, waving his knife along the row of cupboards. Then he waved his fork at the pile of cups on the draining board. "Have some tea and make some toast. There's plenty o' bread."

Even though it was close to their own lunch-times, the Naitabals could never resist Mr Elliott's offers of refreshments, and they spent the next ten minutes organising a pile of toast and marmalade for themselves and big mugs of tea. Mr Elliott had finished by the time they sat down to tuck in, and while he washed his plate in the sink, he asked what was on their minds.

"We were wondering, Mr Elliott," said Jayne, sweetly, "if you know any houses that have a room like this?" She laid the precious sheet of paper on the table and Mr Elliott wandered over with the tea-towel to take a look. "It's this funny corner that makes it very strange – the way it's cut off instead of being square."

Mr Elliott stopped twitching the tea towel in his cup for a second while he looked at the diagram, then burst into a guffaw of laughter.

"Coo!" he said. "Where did you find that?"

"Toby found it in some rubbish," said Ben.

"And you want to find the teddy bear, I suppose?" Mr Elliott went on, still laughing.

29

The Naitabals all suspended their toast-eating for a few moments and stared at him.

"Do you know where it is, then?" said Charlotte.

Mr Elliott laughed again and went back to his washing up. "In the last forty years I reckon I've worked on just about every house in the district," he said. "Well, mates – there's only one house in a ten mile radius that's got a room like that!"

"Where is it, Mr Elliott?" said Jayne, her eyes shining with excitement.

"You won't like it when I tell you!"

"We will – honest we will!"

Mr Elliott guffawed again and clicked his tongue.

"Coo! Now you're talkin'! D'you know why the house I'm thinkin' of has got the corner cut off like that?"

"No, Mr Elliott."

"Well, think. Why would anyone cut a corner off a house?"

"We don't know, Mr Elliott."

"Well, I'll tell you," Mr Elliott went on even before Jayne had finished her answer. "The people that built that extension twenty-five years ago – Smith, their name was. Well, they'd had a pet dog for years they'd loved ever so much, and when it died, they buried it near the house, so's they could be near it, like."

The Naitabals stopped eating again and listened intently as Mr Elliott approached the table.

"A couple o' years later they decided to have an extension built. Now – the walls of the extension were fine – they were just clear o' where the dog was buried. But when I told 'em the *foundations* would disturb the grave, they didn't like it. They said No Way. We talked about it and argued about it, and finally they said, well, the only way we're going to have that extension is if you cut off the corner so's the dog don't get disturbed, like. So that's what we did."

30

"So *you* built it, Mr Elliott!" said Jayne.

"I'm afraid I did, much against me conscience."

"Where is it, Mr Elliott?" said Ben.

"Can't you think o' nowhere yourselves?"

None of them wanted to make any guesses.

"No."

Mr Elliott turned to Charlotte.

"Haven't you never looked out o' your bedroom window and wondered why the corner of someone's house was cut off. . ."

Charlotte thought for a few moments, then stared in horror.

"Oh, no! You don't mean. . .!"

"Well, I can't think of no other house what's got the corner missing. . ."

Charlotte swung towards the others and her voice went off the scale.

"It's true!" she squealed. "One of its corners isn't square! The corner's sort of cut off at an angle!"

"It wasn't my idea," said Mr Elliott, shrugging it off with another chuckle. "I was just followin' instructions, like. . ." He glanced at the diagram again. "And it won't be the downstairs room, neither," he added. "It's a concrete floor. I poured it meself, so there's no way anythin's hidden under there."

The other Naitabals stared at Charlotte.

"It's *Cedric's* house!" she gasped.

31

CHAPTER THREE

The Teddy Bear's Secret

"Not only is it Cedric's *house*," said Charlotte, when they were all back in the Naitabal hut after lunch, "but it's Cedric's *bedroom!*"

"At least that's better than his *parents'* bedroom," said Boff. "That *would* be impossible. At least this way we've got a chance."

"But how on earth can we get into Cedric's house?" said Charlotte. "I've had my brains on the rack for a whole hour, but I can't think of a way we can get in, even for a few seconds. Let alone enough time to go into his room, pull up the carpet and floorboards and go looking underneath for a teddy bear."

"And even if we do find it," said Ben, "how do we get it out of his house without someone asking questions?"

"Come on," prompted Charlotte, glancing at Boff. "Let's have some ideas."

"I have been thinking about it," said Boff apologetically, "but it seems a bit tricky." At almost thirteen, he was the oldest of the Naitabals, and the intellectual leader. He often came up with unexpected ideas when the others failed, so Charlotte was half expecting him to have produced one by now. But no one could think of an answer. How could they penetrate the enemy's castle without raising suspicions?

"We could try the Trojan Horse trick," said Toby, grinning. "We all hide in a big parcel labelled 'Chocolate' and get the postman to deliver us. Then, when Cedric opens it up in his bedroom, we all spring out, tie him up and gag and blindfold him, then take our time looking for the long-lost teddy."

Everyone grinned back, but Toby wasn't expecting anyone to take him seriously.

"We could pretend to make friends with him," suggested Ben. "Then we'd be invited to his house to play games and things."

"Excuse me," said Charlotte, spinning round, "but I think I'm going to be sick." The others laughed as she rushed to the window and pretended to throw up in the Sea of Debris.

"I don't think Charlotte likes that idea," said Toby.

Ben considered.

"How about late at night?" he said, grinning. "Cedric's bound to leave his bedroom window open a bit. We could get one of Mr Elliott's spare ladders over the fence, climb up to his window and get in that way."

"Sounds like a good idea to me," said Jayne, enthused. "Cedric's so thick I bet he sleeps like a baby."

"As long as he doesn't wake up for his two o'clock feed. . ." murmured Charlotte.

"We could probably empty his whole room of furniture," said Toby, "and he wouldn't wake up."

"We could just leave him on the bare floorboards in his Three Little Pigs pyjamas," said Charlotte.

"Or take him outside," said Ben, "and leave him floating on a plank on Charlotte Lagoon."

There was more laughter as they imagined Cedric waking up on Charlotte's pond and wondering how he got there.

"I know it would be bad," said Ben, who was excited at the prospect of an illegal midnight adventure, "but we wouldn't actually be breaking and entering."

"Just entering," said Boff. "That's bad enough."

"And stealing," said Jayne, "if we found the teddy bear."

"Borrowing," said Toby. "We'd only be borrowing it."

No one could think of any other way of getting into Cedric's house to explore, so it was agreed that Ben and

Toby would carry out a night-time raid with the ladder. First, they would wait for news that Cedric was better. Then they would ask their parents' usual permission to sleep in the tree-house. It was quite safe, enclosed by all the surrounding gardens, and they always locked themselves in.

Only two days later, the weather had improved to bright spring sunshine. For the first time since his illness, Cedric appeared in his garden, wrapped (by his mother) in several layers of woollies.

Charlotte saw him over her fence.

"Are you better now, Cedric?" she asked sweetly.

Cedric was flattered.

"Yes, thank you."

"Pity," snapped Charlotte. "It was much nicer when you were ill."

That night, when most people were fast asleep, a shrill bleeping sounded in the Naitabal tree-house, and Ben and Toby sprang to life. Toby was nocturnal and difficult to wake in the mornings, but the small hours were no problem.

"Is that two o'clock?" he whispered.

"Yes."

They climbed out of their sleeping-bags, still fully clothed in Naitabal battledress. They pulled on trainers and stood up. Between them they eased open the trap-door in the roof, climbed through and padlocked it behind them. They crossed the three-rope bridge towards the oak on Boff Island, but jumped down into the Sea of Debris just before they reached the fence. They crossed the sea to Cedric's side and stopped by the aluminium ladder they had placed there earlier in the evening. They had wrapped rags round its feet and at the top so that it would be silent on the ground, and silent when they leaned it against the wall of Cedric's house.

Next, Ben went to check that Cedric's window was open. In the pale light of a crescent moon that was flickering behind thin clouds, he gave the thumbs up. Not only was the

34

window open, but it looked wide enough to get a hand inside. Ben slipped through the loose slats in the fence and on to Pigmo Island.

Between them they managed to pass the ladder over the fence without making any noise, and two minutes later it was in place, resting quietly on its rags on Cedric's window sill.

Toby was dying to do the climbing, but they had already tossed a coin and Ben had won. Toby stood on the bottom rung of the ladder as Ben climbed stealthily towards the sill.

Ben reached carefully inside the lattice window, unhooked the rod that held it firm, then swung it wide open. He attached the rod on the furthest hole and peered past the curtain into the room. The door of the room was slightly ajar, throwing in some light from the hall. Ben breathed a sigh of relief when he saw that it was Cedric's head on the pillow, sleeping peacefully. Cedric was as quiet as Cedric would ever get.

Ben pulled out his Naitabal torch and shone it to his left, into the corner of the room where the cross had been marked on the plan. His heart sank. Right in the same corner stood Cedric's chest of drawers. How could he look under the floorboards when this great thing was standing on top of them?

Ben considered. What would the other Naitabals do? What would Toby have done if he had won the toss instead? He mentally scratched his head, probing for ideas. Suddenly, he knew exactly what the others would have done. He took a deep breath, opened the window wide and climbed in. He knelt down in the corner facing the chest. Carefully, he pulled on both handles of the bottom drawer until it started to slide towards him. It came all the way out without making more than a creak, and he lifted it and placed it carefully on the carpet a little way away.

He crept back and did the same with the next drawer up, placing it quietly on top of the first one. The two small

drawers at the top were easy, and he put those next to the big
ones, one on top of the other. Next, he cleared the top of the
chest: a half-melted plastic model aeroplane, a pile of
comics, a book, *How to Become an Astronaut*, a hopelessly
knotted string puppet, and a picture of Cedric's mother in a
frame.

Ben was pleased. Everything was going smoothly, and he
prepared to move the carcass away from the corner so that he
could get to the carpet and floorboards underneath.

That's when things started to go wrong.

The first sign of trouble was the sound of someone getting
out of bed in the room next to Cedric's. Ben heard the
footsteps padding across the floor, so he quickly ducked
down on the far side of Cedric's bed, just in time to see
Doris through the gap in the door, heading for the bathroom.
He stayed put. Two minutes later, he heard the flush of the
toilet and Doris's returning footsteps.

Then the real horror began. Instead of going past and back
to her own room, Doris pushed open Cedric's door and
headed straight towards the stack of drawers on the floor.
She was half-asleep and running on auto-pilot. She started
to feel the drawers and climb on to them. It was only when
one foot was treading on Cedric's pile of socks that she
opened her eyes properly and let out a whispered curse.

"Hoy! Who's shrugk by bed add takud by battress?" she
said. Unlike Cedric's, her nose was still blocked.

Ben froze.

"Cedrig!" hissed the voice in the nightdress. "Whad hab
you dud with by bed?"

Ben had ducked completely out of sight by this time and
could only guess what was happening. He guessed that she
had woken up a lot more, and that he was in real danger if
she woke Cedric.

What Ben couldn't have known was that Doris's bed had
been in Cedric's room until the night before. She'd become

so used to it that her return trip from the bathroom, half asleep, had taken her straight back to Cedric's room. Now, at last, she was more awake and had realised her mistake.

"Cedrig!" she hissed. "Why hab you got all your drawers out?"

The door had swung almost closed by this time and left the room in virtual darkness. Cedric stirred.

"Who's that?" came his slurred, but near-normal voice.

"Odly be," said Doris.

Ben heard no further conversation. The door opened wide, light from the hall flooded the scene, and Doris's footsteps left the room. The top of Cedric's head appeared as he sat up in bed and looked blankly at the stack of drawers. The bed rocked as he lay down again, turned over, and went back to sleep. The door slowly closed.

Ben waited for the rhythm of Cedric's breathing to steady again, then headed for the window. Even Ben had lost his nerve now. He realised that moving the chest of drawers was one thing, but taking up the carpet and floorboards underneath was quite another. He didn't think it could be done without being discovered. Especially as Cedric was not the heavy sleeper they had hoped for.

Back in the Naitabal hut, Ben explained everything to Toby, and Toby agreed that Ben had done the right thing. It was a good try, but there was no sense in being caught.

Ben grinned as they both kicked off their trainers and slipped inside their sleeping-bags.

"Cedric's going to wonder what on earth happened to his chest of drawers during the night," he said.

Toby grinned back in the darkness.

The other Naitabals were so eager to hear their news, they took Ben and Toby a surprise breakfast the following morning. Toby was successfully woken early by the tempting smell of toasted bacon sandwiches. There were freshly boiled eggs, too, courtesy of Mr Elliott's chickens, who were already clucking in their run down below. When Ben had finished his first round, he related everything that had happened and why he'd eventually given up.

"So how are we going to do it if we can't do it by climbing in his window at night?" said Jayne. "He's not exactly going to invite us up to his room for a game of Snakes and Ladders."

Charlotte had been quiet until that moment, but her face had been growing pinker and pinker. A slightly secret grin had been slowly widening into a huge cheeky one, full of excitement and mischief.

"Wait for it," said Ben, who was the first to notice. "Charlotte's thought of something brilliant."

All heads turned to Charlotte, who couldn't help letting out a brief explosive giggle.

"I *have* thought of something brilliant!" she said, pleased with herself. "I thought it all through last night."

The others listened eagerly as she told them her plan.

When she'd finished, they were all laughing.

At the end she rolled up a sheet of paper like a trumpet and handed it to Ben.

"You'll need that," she said. "That's your secret weapon!"

"That *is* brilliant!" said Boff, grinning.

CHAPTER FOUR

Charlotte's Secret

Later that morning Charlotte settled down by the pond in her garden (it was Charlotte Lagoon to the Naitabals), and watched her seven-year-old brother Harry launching his toy submarine.

Next door, she heard the sounds of the other two Igmopong arriving at Cedric and Doris's front door. Presently they appeared, Andy Wilson thin and white like a pipe cleaner, and his sister Amanda. She was dressed all in green and looked like an aubergine. The four Igmopong came rushing out of Cedric's back door and down through Pigmo Island, heading for their tree-house.

"Cedric," Charlotte called sweetly as they passed.

Cedric stopped dead and the others piled into the back of him.

"What?" he said, turning. He pushed the others out of his way so he could see her.

"Could you please do me a favour?"

Cedric knew from long experience that whatever answer he gave, Charlotte would probably retort with "lie down on a railway line" or "get a job as a Kamikaze pilot" or some other insult.

"No," he said. Then, before she could speak, he added quickly, "But you can do me one. Go and tie yourself to a lightning rod and wait for a thunderstorm."

The other three Igmopong sniggered.

"I'd be ever so grateful if you could do me this favour," Charlotte repeated, ignoring the insult and oozing charm.

"How grateful?" demanded Doris. "I bet you wouldn't be

ten pounds grateful."

"Or a night in your tree-house grateful," said Amanda, seeing an opportunity.

"Or two nights," said Cedric.

"Or a hundred," said Andy.

"It's not that sort of favour," said Charlotte. "It's something really important, which is why I wanted you to do it." Charlotte turned and started walking away, speaking to them over her shoulder. "But if you don't want to do it, I'll ask someone else."

It worked. Cedric's curiosity got the better of him.

"I didn't say I *wouldn't* do it," he said quickly. "I don't even know what it is yet, do I?"

Charlotte turned to face them again.

"You've got to say you'll do it first – before I tell you what it is."

"Oh yes," scoffed Doris. "And then you'll tell him to put his head in a microwave."

"No I won't," Charlotte promised.

"Why have I got to say first, before you tell me what it is?" said Cedric.

"Because. . ." Charlotte hesitated, thinking quickly, "because it's a *secret*, that's why. I'm not going to tell you the secret and then have you saying you don't want to do it."

Cedric put on a crafty look.

"Okay," he said. "I'll do it."

Charlotte saw the look and knew what Cedric was thinking.

"If I tell you the secret and you *don't* do it," she said, "I'll – " she was suddenly brilliantly inspired again – "I'll use my magic powers on you."

Cedric scoffed.

"What magic powers?"

"Magic powers to *make a mess of your bedroom*. I can move things around just using my mind. Especially in

40

bedrooms at night."

Cedric's jaw dropped open. Behind him, Doris turned a bright red.

"I can, you know," said Charlotte. "I've already practised it once – to make sure – in case I told you the secret and then you double-crossed me."

"H-how did you practise it?" said Cedric, aghast.

"I imagined a chest of drawers – *you have got a chest of drawers, haven't you?* – I imagined a chest of drawers and focused my mind on your bedroom. Yours *is* that one there, isn't it? Nearest my house?" She pointed.

"Y-yes."

"And then – " Charlotte fixed Cedric with a witchy stare, "– and then I pulled the drawers out one by one and moved them across the room."

Cedric let out an audible gasp.

"I've done it before," Charlotte went on relentlessly, "to my – my cousin – so I know it works. But of course, I made much more of a mess of *her* room." Her face changed to a look of pure evil. "*Serve her right.*"

"W-what did you do?" stuttered Cedric.

"I piled all her furniture against the door so no one could get in to help her. Then I threw all her favourite things out of the window and *turned her bed upside down with her still in it*, asleep."

"I bet you didn't," said Doris, but her voice was less forceful than usual.

"I can prove it if you like," said Charlotte. "I'll do it to you."

"N-no," said Cedric. "That's okay."

"Did it work yesterday?"

"Did what work yesterday?"

"Last night. When I moved the drawers out of your chest of drawers?"

"N-no," said Cedric, lying badly. He glared back at Doris.

"No, nothing happened last night. It didn't work."

Charlotte penetrated Cedric's eyes with another witchy stare.

"I think you're *lying*, Cedric," she said. Cedric's eyes bulged as he stared back at her. "You *are* lying, Cedric, aren't you? I *know* you are."

For once, Cedric and Doris were bereft of speech. Suddenly, Charlotte relaxed her look and added, "Do you want to do this favour, or not?"

Cedric, trying to look unconcerned, grew pink. He thought for a few seconds while he recovered himself.

"Yes," he said. "Yes, I'll do the favour. What is it? And what's the secret?"

"And you promise to do the favour after I tell you the secret?"

"Yes."

"It's quite a big favour, actually."

"That's all right," said Cedric, who was burning to know what the secret was so much by now, he'd have said yes to anything.

"Well – the secret is this cousin of mine. The one I turned upside down in her bed."

"What about her?"

"She's coming to stay for a few days."

"That's not much of a secret," spat Doris. "It's just about the most pathetic secret I've ever heard anyone tell in the whole of my life."

"Yes," said Amanda. "Mine too."

"Yeah," said Andy.

"That isn't the secret part," said Charlotte calmly. "And if the rest of you are just going to be your usual *stupidness* and heckle, perhaps I should just tell Cedric – in private?"

"No," said Doris hastily. "You can tell all of us. We won't say anything."

"Well," said Charlotte, "she's coming to stay for a few

42

days, and you've probably guessed already – *I hate her*. The *secret* is. . ." Charlotte took a few steps towards them again and leaned over the fence confidentially. "The secret is that everyone calls her my 'cousin' – *but she's really my identical twin sister*!"

"How can she be?" said Doris in a loud voice. "She'd be living here with you if she was your twin sister."

"Sshh! Keep your voice down," said Charlotte. "I'm not going to tell you any more if you're going to ruin it by shouting everything."

"I won't shout," said Doris, then added, "as long as nothing's stupid."

"I can see I'll have to tell you the whole story," Charlotte continued. She leaned in closer. "My mother thought she couldn't have children, and my Aunt Susan didn't want any children at all. So when my Aunt Susan suddenly had twins, she decided to keep one and give the other one to my mother."

Cedric's mouth shot open like the entrance to a pothole.

"You mean Mrs Maddison isn't your real mother, then?" he said, aghast.

"That's right. That's why it's such a secret."

"What about Harry?" said Doris. She indicated Charlotte's brother, who was dragging the pond again for his toy submarine.

"Oh, he's a twin as well," said Charlotte, deciding she might as well go the whole hog. "Aunt Susan had another set of twins a few years later and gave us one of those as well."

"Is Harry's twin coming to stay at the same time?"

"I'm not sure," said Charlotte. "He's going to stay with another aunt at some stage. He does come here occasionally, but they always just swap them. It isn't always Harry you see in the garden here. Sometimes it's Billy."

Charlotte had been told that children got a dark spot on

their heart every time they told a lie. At this rate, she thought, hers would be completely black by lunch-time.

"Is that Harry now?" said Amanda.

Charlotte called.

"Harry!"

Harry looked up.

"Yes," said Charlotte. "Yes, it is. I can't tell them apart either." She plunged on.

"I didn't meet my twin again until we were seven, and we hated each other straight away. We look the same, but we're *completely* different people. And now she's got to stay with us for a few days because her mother – our mother – has to go into hospital, and her father – sorry, *our* father – is at work all day. They might bring Billy as well while they're coming," she added nonchalantly.

Cedric's mouth was still gaping wide like Cheddar Gorge.

"So what's the favour?" he said, closing it at last.

"Well – we hate each other. I don't want her anywhere near me, and she doesn't want to come here and stay, either. But we've no choice."

"Can't she stay where Harry goes?" said Doris.

"No. Harry may not go. Anyway," she added, "they hate each other as well."

"So?" said Cedric. "I still don't know what the favour is."

"I just wondered if you could have her with you most of the time," said Charlotte. "I know you don't like me, but you'll probably like Margery a lot. She could even join your gang if you'd let her."

"Margery?"

"That's her name," said Charlotte. "Pathetic, isn't it? I'd kill myself if I had to grow up with a name like that."

"I like it," said Doris stiffly. "It's my middle name."

"Oh, sorry, Doris. But she always wears *red dresses*. She won't wear anything else. Can you believe it?"

"I like red as well," said Doris tartly. She was wearing a

red top at that moment, which clashed spectacularly with her ginger hair.

"She wears her hair down, which doesn't suit our face at all," Charlotte went on. "But her face is slightly fatter, so perhaps it doesn't notice much. But will you look after her for me, and keep her out of my way?"

"Okay," said Cedric. "We'll see what she's like, and if we like her, she can spend some time with us."

"But if we don't like her – " warned Doris, "if she's anything like you, for instance – you can have her back and serve you right."

"Thanks," said Charlotte sweetly. "That's taken a big problem off my mind. I don't even want to see her when she arrives, so I'll make myself scarce. I'll get Mum – er, Mrs Maddison – to send her round."

"Okay," said Cedric.

Charlotte walked away, towards Harry, as Doris turned to Cedric, looking furious.

"I *told* you it wasn't me who moved your stupid drawers!" she snarled viciously.

Cedric clenched his teeth back at her.

"And I told *you* it wasn't *me*!"

Charlotte realised that the hardest part of her plan was going to be getting her seven-year-old brother Harry's co-operation. She wondered if it would be better if he was told the missing twin story as if it was real, or if he could be trusted to go along with the joke.

"Harry," she said at last.

Harry was still in the pond, so confidential conversation was not really possible. Harry's legs were caked with mud up to the knees, and his hands and arms were caked with mud up to the elbows. He stooped down and scooped out another double handful of black slime and examined it closely.

"What are you looking for, Harry?"

"Deaf charges," said Harry without looking up.

"I thought you were looking for your submarine?"

"No. Found that. Lookin' for deaf charges."

"I think you mean *depth* charges, Harry."

Charlotte remembered now. Harry's game involved floating his toy submarine on the pond and then throwing glass marbles (deaf charges) at it until it sank. She now learned that he had recovered the sub and nineteen marbles, but there was still one missing.

"I want to talk to you, Harry. If you come out now I'll *give* you five more marbles to make up for the one you've lost." (Charlotte had been teaching Harry the evils of betting the week before, and had won half his marbles in a game of poker.)

Harry came out of the pond. Charlotte made him wash off the worst of the mud before going into the house. His pockets bulged with one submarine and nineteen marbles, but at least he'd had the sense to rinse them before stuffing them in.

Charlotte sighed. Back in the kitchen, she stood him in the middle where he couldn't make anything dirty, and started to explain her plan. She'd decided on the truth.

"Would you like to help me play a trick on the Igmopong?" she began.

Harry nodded.

"Yes."

"I'm going to pretend that I've got a twin sister called Margery, and I'm going to pretend that I'm her – okay?"

Harry nodded.

"Yes."

"Now Margery only wears red dresses, and she always has her hair down – not in a pony tail like mine. And she has a slightly fatter face. So every time you see me in a red dress with my hair down, that's when I'm Margery. Okay?"

Harry nodded vigorously. He liked the funny feeling it gave him and carried on nodding even more vigorously until he nearly fell over and Charlotte had to grab him by his neck to stop him.

"Don't do that, Harry. You'll rattle your brains out."

"Are you Margery now?"

Charlotte sighed again.

"Am I wearing a red dress?"

Harry looked, frowning.

"No."

"I'm not Margery, then, am I? Is my hair hanging down?"

Harry looked.

"Yes."

"No, it isn't."

"Yes it is."

"Where?"

"There!" Harry grabbed a single hair that had escaped Charlotte's pony tail band and pulled it out.

"Ow! That's *one* hair hanging down, Harry, not *all* my hair. Now don't be silly. Pony tail equals Charlotte. No pony tail equals Margery. Got it?"

"Yes." Harry remembered something else. "And a fat face."

"Yes. And there's another thing as well."

"Wot?"

"We've changed your name to Billy for a few days."

Harry raised his eyebrows and grinned.

"Goodee!" he said. "I like Billy!"

Charlotte realised it was a good moment to clean Harry up and change his clothes before he went out again as Billy.

Her next problem was the grown-ups, although perhaps it wasn't much of a problem. Her parents rarely spoke to Mr and Mrs Morgan, even though they were next-door neighbours, so there wasn't much chance of them accidentally finding out the truth. Satisfied, she went two

47

doors along to tell Mr Elliott, whom she'd just heard arriving home in his boneshaker van. Mr Elliott was very bright, of course, and never missed a trick.

"Coo!" he said. "So that's how you're going to get the teddy bear! Good luck, mate!"

At last everything was ready. After lunch, Charlotte climbed the stairs to her bedroom, crossed to the wardrobe, and took out the bright red dress that she hated and had never worn. She put it on, then took her hair out of its pony tail, shook it out on to her shoulders and brushed it. She changed her shoes and socks, pushed flattened pieces of cotton wool into her cheeks and stood looking at herself in the mirror.

She scowled at herself.

"Hello, Margery," she said.

CHAPTER FIVE

Margery

In the kitchen, Charlotte found Harry, freshly smartened up, waiting patiently for his five marbles.

"Hello, Billy," she said. "Do you know who I am?"

Harry checked Charlotte's dress and Charlotte's hair and Charlotte's fatter face.

"Marjelly," he said.

Charlotte sighed.

"Margery."

"Marge*ree*," crooned Harry.

"Well done, Billy. Here, you can have *ten* marbles for being so clever."

"Thanks!"

Charlotte stood aside to avoid being barged by Harry's solid body as he shot into the garden, then followed him down the steps into the open air.

"Don't go into the pond with your clean things on, Billy!" she called. It was like asking a lion to be kind to zebras: within seconds he was in the pond with his shoes and socks off, looking for his lost marble.

Charlotte walked past him, flicking her long hair and swirling her red dress. She felt different. She wasn't Charlotte any more. She wasn't a Naitabal. She hated Charlotte and the other Naitabals. She was an Igmopong. She continued down Charlotte Island with a little high-stepping walk, her nose held a little higher in the air. She sensed the four Igmopong huddled in their pathetic tree-house, pressed against each other and clinging to the branches of the tree to stop themselves sliding down the sloping floor and falling out. She stopped nearby and looked up.

"Hello," she said in a slightly rougher, more hollow voice than usual, partly thanks to the cotton wool. "Who are you?"

"I'm Cedric," said Cedric.

"I'm Margery," said Charlotte. "It's nice to meet you." She clapped her hands together and let out a little squeal. "I *love* your tree-house! It's brilliant! Did you build it all yourselves?"

"Yes," said Cedric. His chest swelled with pride. "This is my sister, Doris."

"Hello, Doris."

"We *all* built it," said Doris.

"I *love* your red top, Doris!" said Charlotte. Internally, she was already throwing up.

"This is Amanda, and this is her brother Andy."

They said hello and Charlotte resumed her survey of their tree-house.

"Your tree-house is much more exciting than *Charlotte's*," she said. "They had theirs built for them, but it looks like a block of flats, doesn't it? Yours looks like a *real* tree-house!"

Cedric agreed that the Naitabal tree-house did remind him of a block of flats. It was funny that he hadn't noticed it before.

"Where's Charlotte?" said Doris.

"Oh, the big baby's up in her bedroom, sulking," said Charlotte. "She hates me and I hate her and she couldn't bear me coming to stay, so she kicked up a tantrum and hid herself away. That's typical Charlotte, though, isn't it? I bet you must hate her as well? And those stuffy friends of hers. . ."

"We do," said Cedric, intrigued. He kept looking at this girl called Margery who looked almost identical to Charlotte (except that she *was* just a little fatter in the face), and yet was so much nicer. "We think they're all stupid," he went

50

on. "All they ever do is sit in their silly block of flats all day and play games. But we go out in the real woods and make rafts and things."

"Wow! Have you got a raft?"

"Well. . . it sank. But we're going to make a submarine soon. There's something at the bottom of. . ."

He received a smart kick from Doris and stopped.

Charlotte turned towards the Naitabal hut again, knowing that the other four Naitabals were probably lying on the floor out of sight, killing themselves with laughter as they overheard the conversation.

"I don't like any of the Naitabals," she said. "Especially Charlotte."

"I don't like Charlotte," said Amanda. "She's stuck up."

"And selfish," said Charlotte.

"And ugly," said Cedric.

Charlotte stiffened.

"Do you think I'm ugly, too, then?" she said.

Cedric looked at her guiltily.

"Er – no – of course not."

"But I look exactly like Charlotte."

"Yes, but – " Cedric seemed to be struggling for words for a moment, then found inspiration. "It's not her *face* that's ugly, it's the. . . way she holds it. She holds it ugly."

"Like this?" said Charlotte, pulling the sort of face she usually reserved for Cedric.

Cedric was horrified at the likeness.

"Yes," he said, shocked. "Exactly like that."

"What are you planning at the moment?" said Charlotte. "Anything exciting that I can join in?"

"We *are* planning something," said Doris, before Cedric could say anything, "but it's still a secret. We might tell you when we've known you a bit longer."

Charlotte moved right up to the fence and whispered across the gap between herself and the Igmopong's tree-house.

51

"I might be able to tell you some of the Naitabals' secrets," she said.

The Igmopong had a hurried, huddled conversation, and when they had finished, Cedric looked down at her.

"You'd better come up," he said.

Charlotte could hardly believe her luck. Suddenly, she had gained access to one of the Igmopong's most precious secrets, their tree-house. (Using it as the jail for Monopoly when they were ill didn't count.) It was surely only a matter of time before she would gain access to an even more secret sanctuary – Cedric's bedroom – and the floorboards beneath Cedric's carpet.

"And all of this," she was thinking, "just for a teddy bear."

Charlotte climbed the short knotted rope that led into the Igmopong's tree-house. She'd had some practice when she'd been sent to jail during their last game of Monopoly. She squeezed herself into the last space left on the sloping floor, then took hold of a branch to prevent herself falling out. It wasn't very far from the ground, and it was low enough to jump down.

"I like it in here," she said. She was so close to the Igmopong now, in the middle, that she could feel four lots of hot breath breathing on her from four different directions. "Much better than *their* place. This is a *real* tree-house."

"Tell us some of their secrets, then," said Doris, without wasting any time. Doris was suspicious by nature, but right now she was even more suspicious than usual. "What are they planning?"

Charlotte turned her head in a quick movement, flicking her long hair and liking the feel of it. She had already thought about what 'secrets' she would give away. It didn't come easily, but she managed to smile sweetly at Doris.

"Charlotte's got magic powers," she said. "She can move furniture without being in the same room." Charlotte looked round at the awestruck faces. "I say, she hasn't moved any of *yours*, has she?"

Cedric and Doris exchanged glances.

"We think she *might* have," said Cedric. "Only I thought Doris had done it."

"Yes, he accused *me*," said Doris. "But I knew he must have done it himself."

"But I didn't," said Cedric.

"What was moved?" said Charlotte.

"My chest of drawers."

"Sounds like Charlotte," said Charlotte, lowering her voice to a whisper. She casually yawned and raised her free arm straight up in the air as if stretching. "There's another secret, too."

Up in the Naitabal hut, Ben saw Charlotte's signal and grabbed the paper trumpet she had given him.

"We already knew the one you've just told us," Doris interrupted. "Tell us a better one."

Charlotte pointed towards the Naitabal tree-house.

"You see that trumpet thing that one of them's putting out of the window?"

The Igmopong turned.

"Yes."

"Well – that's a listening device."

"What do you mean?" said Doris.

"Well." Charlotte lowered her voice. "When that's out of the window, the Naitabals can hear everything we're saying. It magnifies the sound by twenty. It's just as if we're shouting."

Andy suddenly looked scared.

"It's out of the window now!" he said in a hiss.

"Oh, well done, Andy," said Doris. "We have got eyes as well, you know."

"That means they can hear us now," said Cedric, worried.

"There's an easy way to stop them using it," said Charlotte.

53

"How?" said Cedric. He leaned forward and breathed hot, excited breath all over her face.

"That's another of their secrets," she said, "but I'll tell you, as you're my friends."

Cedric smiled an oily smile of gratitude that made Charlotte want to throw up. She pressed on, lowering her voice to the lowest of whispers.

"Well, think about it. That tube multiplies the sound by twenty and makes everything as clear as if we were shouting it. So if we *shout*, it'll *deafen* them!"

The Igmopong grinned. Without waiting another moment, Cedric turned and shouted towards the paper trumpet that Ben was pointing through the window in their direction. As Cedric's stream of abuse rent the air, they saw Ben drop the trumpet and clap his hands to his ears.

Cedric and the Igmopong were impressed.

"Stupid old Naitabals!" he finished, at the top of his voice.

"Told you," said Charlotte, simply. "Now – is there somewhere *private* we can talk?"

Cedric considered.

"My bedroom's the best place," he announced. "We can keep an eye on the Naitabals from there, and they won't be able to hear *anything*."

"Good," said Charlotte. "Anyway, I'd like to see what Charlotte did with your chest of drawers."

"Come on then," said Cedric. "Let's go."

There was a general scramble to leave the tree-house, and Charlotte breathed a word of warning before they started off towards the house.

"There's one other thing," she said. "Another secret. If your mother sees me, you must call me Charlotte. We're not allowed to tell anyone outside the family about us being twins."

"Okay."

As the Igmopong and Charlotte moved off, Boff, Jayne,

Ben and Toby were on the floor of the Naitabal hut, heads below window height, creasing themselves with laughter.

Mrs Morgan was in her kitchen as the motley crocodile of children wound through.

"Oh, hello, Charlotte," she said, as Charlotte appeared at the end of the line. "How nice to see you playing with Doris and Cedric and their friends for a change."

"Yes," said Charlotte, winking at the others. Cedric and Andy winked back, except that Andy couldn't wink, so blinked twice instead.

"I'm always saying to my darling Cedric and Doris they should be more friendly with you. . ."

Mrs Morgan's voice faded into a drone as Charlotte followed the others up the stairs.

Cedric's bedroom was exactly as Ben had described it. There on the right, opposite the door, stood the chest of drawers, exactly above the spot where the diagram showed the hidden teddy bear to be. The wall behind it wasn't like a normal corner. It was as if it had been curtained off, or as if it was a corner cupboard without a door. But as Mr Elliott had told them, it had been built like that for a very peculiar reason.

"So this is your room," she said.

The four Igmopong stood aside to allow Margery to see the room, and now they were waiting for her verdict.

"It's lovely," Charlotte said at last. "I love the big red roses on the wallpaper. Did you choose it, Cedric?"

"Yes – well, my mother helped me."

"And I *love* the way it *clashes* with the zig-zag pattern on the curtains. Did you choose them as well?"

"No, I did," snapped Doris. "Cedric's no good at choosing curtains."

"I love everything," Charlotte continued, acting her heart out to look enthusiastic. "The bed, the carpet, the window, the aeroplane mobiles, the—" she stopped suddenly, her attention focused on the chest of drawers.

The four Igmopong watched her as her eyes travelled up and down the set of drawers and from one side of the room to the other.

"Is that the chest that Charlotte moved?" Charlotte continued suddenly.

"Yes," said Cedric. "She made all the drawers come out and threw them over there – " He pointed. "And—"

"I know how to stop her doing it again," Charlotte butted in.

"How?" said Doris.

"Charlotte can only move things from south to north. She uses the power of the earth's compass," added Charlotte, improvising wildly. "That's north, isn't it?" She pointed to normal corner to the left of the window. "So if you move the chest of drawers into *that* corner, she won't be able to move it any further."

"Do you think so?"

"I know so. She's my twin, isn't she? I know her better than anyone."

"Let's do it," said Cedric.

"Yeah," said Andy.

Minutes later the chest of drawers had been moved. Charlotte smiled to herself as she stared at the dirty patch of carpet where it had been standing. So far, so good. At least the chest of drawers was out of the way. Now all that stood between her and the secret hiding place was a patch of dirty carpet and some floorboards.

"Come on," she said brightly. "Where's your vacuum cleaner? Let's get rid of this horrid germ-filled dust."

Cedric fetched the cleaner and the deed was done in no time. Charlotte stood admiring the room. Inside, she was thinking what a tasteless mess it was.

"There!" she said. "I think your room's absolutely perfect now. Don't change anything, ever!"

Andy and Amanda nodded in agreement as Cedric beamed with pleasure. Doris wasn't exactly smiling, but was carefully watching their guest.

Charlotte couldn't see a way of getting at the floorboards for the moment, so she made her excuses and started to leave.

Suddenly, Doris spoke.

"Margery. . ."

Charlotte almost forgot to answer to the name, but remembered a few split seconds late, and turned.

"Yes?"

"I thought you and Charlotte said this was supposed to be a big secret – about her having a twin?"

"Yes, it is. No one else must know."

"So how come Charlotte and you are both here together, then?"

Charlotte turned her head casually back towards the door.

"We're both *here*," she said, continuing out of the room. "But we're not allowed *out* together. Not that I'd *want* to be out with Charlotte. We take it in turns. That's why I've got to go back. To let Charlotte out."

The Igmopong escorted her down through the empty kitchen and out into the back garden. She scaled the fence on to Charlotte Island, where Harry was still standing in the pond. As Charlotte disappeared towards her house, Amanda and Doris wandered over, and Doris spoke to Harry.

"Harry," she called quietly, "who's that going into your house?"

Harry didn't bother to look up, but shouted in an annoyed scream. Harry had two voices: a normal one, and a ninety decibel bellow. There was no in-between, and the bellow never needed building up. It was a bellow straight away.

Doris saw him snatching a lungful of breath and she and Amanda covered their ears just in time.

"I'M. . . NOT. . . HARRY. . . I'M. . . BILLY!"

Doris uncovered her ears and asked the question again.

"Sorry – Billy. Who's that going into your house?" She hastily blocked her ears again before Harry answered.

"MY. . . SISTER!"

"I KNOW she's your sister, Billy, but WHAT'S HER NAME?"

Harry glanced at Charlotte's disappearing form and checked the hair and the dress. He then took a huge lungful of air and gave full vent to each individual syllable.

"MAR. . . GER. . . REE!" he screamed.

At last, though half deafened, even the highly suspicious Doris seemed satisfied.

CHAPTER SIX

Charlotte's Magic

Back in her own house, Charlotte ran up the stairs to her bedroom, and almost bumped into her mother. Mrs Maddison stood aside to let the flash of red pass, then stared after her daughter wide-eyed with amusement.

"Charlotte, whatever—" she started to say, then changed it to, "I thought you hated that dress. . . And what have you done to your hair. . .?"

"Just playing a game," explained Charlotte, grinning, as Mrs Maddison shook her head and went downstairs murmuring, "Whatever next. . ."

Charlotte changed rapidly from Margery red dress to Charlotte jeans and was halfway through putting her hair back into a Charlotte pony tail when she had another brilliant idea. She'd been wracking her brains the whole time she was in Cedric's room, wondering how on earth she was going to get the teddy bear. Moving his furniture had been easy, but taking up his floorboards – that was much more difficult. Then she heard the sound of Mr Morgan's car starting up, and rushed to her parents' front bedroom window to see who was in it. It was only Mr and Mrs Morgan, going shopping. And suddenly it came to her. She'd already sown the seed – all she needed to do was gather the crop!

Full of new excitement, she changed back into Margery.

"Sorry, Charlotte," she said aloud. "You'll just have to stay in a bit longer."

She glanced quickly in the full length mirror on her wardrobe to make sure Margery was complete, then skipped down to the kitchen and took out a small onion. Just then Harry came in the back door.

"You were brilliant, Harry," she began, then saw his chest filling with air ready to protest. She quickly clapped a hand over his mouth. "I know – you're Billy. But you can be Harry again now."

"But you're Margery," he protested.

"Yes, I'm still Margery for a little while. But you be Harry now. Confuse the Igmopong."

Harry nodded violently and ran off to the toilet, shouting, "Goodee, I'm Harry again! Hooray! Harr-ay!"

His voice faded from Charlotte's mind. She took the onion, cut off the root end, and then cut off a thick slice. She put cling film on the remaining onion, put it back in the vegetable rack and took the slice and chopped it up. She put her face near the chopping board and breathed in the prickly fumes. As soon as her eyes were stinging and beginning to run with tears, she hurled herself out of the back door, flung herself against the Igmopong's fence, and buried her head in her arms, sobbing loudly with big theatrical heaves of her shoulders.

The Igmopong, who were hovering halfway down Pigmo Island, came towards her. At the same moment, Harry came out of the back door, slammed it, and tore past Charlotte towards the pond.

"What's the matter with Margery, Billy?" said Amanda.

Harry stopped in his tracks and glared at her, screamed "NOT BILLY! HARRY!" then accelerated again towards the pond.

Amanda stared at the retreating bullet. He was wearing exactly the same clothes as Billy, and even had the same mud patterns on the same knees. She couldn't see any difference at all. But the distressing sound of Margery sobbing was more interesting, and Amanda shrugged and followed the other Igmopong to where Charlotte was draped over the fence in abject sorrow.

"What's the matter?" said Cedric.

"It's that horrid Charlotte!" said Charlotte, letting out an extra big sob and taking in a long sniff. "She's just worked her magic on *me*!"

"What's she done?"

"She says she saw me talking to you in your tree-house, and she's so cross she's magicked my favourite teddy bear away." She sobbed again.

"What – just made it disappear?"

"Worse than that," wailed Charlotte.

"How worse?" said Doris.

"She's made it go *under the floorboards* in Cedric's bedroom."

The Igmopong stared in disbelief. It was incredible. Even Doris looked impressed with the absent Charlotte's powers.

"It's not possible," said Amanda, although she'd already seen Billy turn seamlessly into Harry. "No one could do that. Not even a magician on the telly."

"No," said Andy. "Not even a magician in real life."

"Well," sniffed Charlotte, "Charlotte has. She's moved it from south to north, see? Like I said she could. From her house to yours."

Cedric paled.

"That means she could move my chest of drawers to Mr Elliott's house," he said, alarmed.

"It's too big," said Charlotte. "She can slide something like that in a room, but not fly it. She can only fly little things across from one house to another. Like a teddy bear."

"I don't believe it," said Doris at last, after thinking about it. Her natural suspicions weren't satisfied. "No one could *really* do that."

Charlotte rubbed her eyes and looked up.

"She can. She *has*. It's gone."

"She's just hidden it," said Doris.

"Why don't we go and have a look?" said Cedric.

Charlotte brightened and wiped her cheeks.

"Could we?"

"Come on."

Cedric led off towards the house while Charlotte followed, mopping her eyes with a tissue.

Up in Cedric's bedroom, the Igmopong piled in behind him. As Charlotte joined them, Cedric spoke.

"Did she say where, exactly?"

"Yes," said Charlotte. "Where the chest of drawers was."

Cedric moved to the corner, followed by his gang, with Charlotte bringing up the rear. She pushed her way through to the front as Cedric tugged the carpet off its gripper strips and folded the cut-off corner outwards to reveal the floorboards underneath.

It was immediately obvious to Charlotte that the floorboards had been taken up in the past. Two of the long ones that went towards the corner had been sawn across. The two shortened pieces resembled a trap-door that had been screwed back into place – not nailed like the other floorboards.

Charlotte's heart started thumping as she realised what she was looking at. She had no doubt that it was the hiding place of the teddy bear on the diagram that Jayne and Toby had found at Deep Shadow Cottage.

"We need a screwdriver," she said, excited, taking charge. "Can you get one, Cedric?"

"I know where there's one," he said, and ran off.

Half a minute later he was back. Charlotte grabbed the screwdriver from him and started to undo the screws one by one, placing them to one side. Each little plank had four screws, two for each joist, and it took a long time for all eight to come out. Charlotte crouched above the space with her back to the others so they couldn't see anything much before she did. As the last screw came out, she used the screwdriver to lever open the two loose pieces of floor like double swing doors. She held her breath as she lifted them up and peered through the widening crack in the middle.

In the end, she almost didn't expect to find the teddy bear. Part of her thought the whole thing must be a hoax, and another part of her thought the teddy bear, if there was one, would have been found years ago. But as the light flooded into the gap and showed a hint of shining metal and sharp angles, it almost took her breath away completely.

It was a light oak box. It sat between the joists, measured about thirty centimetres long, and was strengthened with metal straps like a pirate's treasure chest. The edges of the lid were decorated with silhouettes of fifteen pirate figures burned into the wood. Charlotte tried to shield it from the Igmopong as she read the words branded on to the lid across the middle, 'SARAH'S LITTLE TREASURE'.

She quickly reached through the gap in the floorboards and tugged at the lid, covering the inscription with her hand before the others could see it. The box wasn't locked, and the lid flipped open easily.

Inside was the teddy bear.

It lay on its back, dark brown, with brown glass-button eyes staring blankly up at her, a red ribbon round its neck, and a calm smile curled under its black shiny nose. There was nothing else in the hole.

"It's here!" she shouted. "It *is* here, look!" She pushed the two pieces of floorboard to one side and moved round to allow the others a proper look. Before any of them could touch it, she lifted it out and hugged it to her chest, at the same time feeling the crinkle of paper pinned to its back.

"Thank you, Cedric!" she breathed. "I'm so pleased to have him back!"

Cedric, Doris, Andy and Amanda were all dumbfounded. There couldn't have been any trickery. The chest of drawers had been standing on the space for donkeys years until twenty minutes ago, and they'd all been there when it had been moved. Why, they'd moved it themselves. Margery had been with them the whole time, and no one had gone into Cedric's room in the short time Margery had gone back into Charlotte's house. It was a miracle. Charlotte really *was* magic.

But Doris, though dumbfounded at finding the teddy, was nosey and suspicious, and had made sure she missed nothing as Charlotte opened the hole. She had glimpsed something written on the little wooden chest.

"What was that message on top of the box?" she barked. "You opened it too quick for me to see it."

Charlotte was already frantically thinking, wondering if she could come up with something convincing. Even as Doris kicked the lid shut with her foot, and chanted 'SARAH'S LITTLE TREASURE' in a sarcastic voice, inspiration came to Charlotte. She screwed up her nose into a look of annoyance.

"That's my middle name!" she complained. "Charlotte knows I hate it, and she's put it on the lid on purpose!"

"And what's that paper on its back?" added Doris, who hadn't missed anything.

Charlotte was already dreading what it might say – dreading that it might give something away. But before she could make an excuse and escape without showing it to them, Doris had snatched the sheet and read it out.

"*With love from Deedy.*"

Charlotte grabbed the sheet back, muttering lamely that there were two D's in Charlotte Maddison. It was Charlotte's secret name for herself, she added. She hastily recovered the chest, then thanked them all again. She asked Cedric sweetly if he'd mind *awfully* putting the floorboards back, then she made a hasty departure before any of them came out of their trance and started asking any more awkward questions.

Back in her room, breathing a huge sigh of relief, she changed from Margery to Charlotte in two minutes flat. Then, with the teddy bear in its chest in a carrier bag, she trotted down to the Naitabal tree-house to tell her story.

When Charlotte had finished bringing the Naitabals up to date with her news, and they'd finished laughing at the stupidity of the Igmopong, they were all anxious to see the teddy bear.

"I still can't believe it was really there," said Charlotte, "but look." She reached for the plastic bag that she'd placed in the middle of the floor, and slowly removed the chest.

"A pirate's treasure chest!" said Jayne, feeling the lid. "Look at all the lovely pirates!"

Charlotte opened the lid and produced the teddy bear. "Isn't he lovely?"

The teddy bear was handed round for everyone to see. Boff was the last to handle it. He turned it over and round and round, squinting at every detail.

"What are you looking for, Boff?" said Ben.

Boff peered over the top of his glasses at Ben.

"I don't think anyone would go to all that trouble to hide a teddy bear in someone else's house for years and draw a plan and write 'teddy bear hidden here' on it unless it was really important, do you?" he said. He looked at the little wooden chest. "And 'Sarah's Little Treasure' is a bit intriguing, too."

"I wonder who Sarah is?" said Jayne. "Do you think the teddy was hers?"

"Must have been," said Charlotte.

Boff found a small silk label with washing instructions sticking out of the seam in one leg, but that was the only other clue. There was no maker's name, and no sign of what Boff was really looking for.

"There's no zip," he said, offering it to the others. "We

65

need a surgeon. Who's good at opening teddy bears' stomachs?"

"Boff!" Jayne protested, grabbing and hugging it. "You can't cut him open!"

"But there must be something hidden inside. Otherwise, why would this 'Deedy' hide it?"

"Boff's right," said Ben. "I squeezed it quite a lot, and there's something crackly in there. It might be a sheet of paper – or – " he grinned in delight – "it might be *money*!"

"But we can't cut him open!" said Jayne, giving it a last hug.

"There's a seam down the back," said Charlotte. "All we've got to do is slit the stitches. We can easily sew it up again afterwards."

"That sounds a good idea," said Toby. "Come on, let's operate!"

As Charlotte had been the one clever enough to trick the Igmopong to get it, and as she seemed to know teddy bear anatomy better than the others, she was voted top surgeon. Moments later, she was using Ben's penknife to cut and unpick the stitches down the bear's spine. She didn't need to go all the way. As soon as the gap was a few centimetres long, she explored the teddy's interior with eyes and fingers, and soon winkled out a little rolled up sheet of paper.

Now everyone was really excited. Charlotte dumped the teddy unceremoniously face down on the floor and unrolled the paper. She spread it out for the others to see as she read it out aloud:

"Go to the top of my nest, as low as you can be,
  In limb, o hollow chest, one, two, three."

"It's obviously a riddle," said Jayne. "But what does it mean?"

"Nest must mean house," said Ben straight away.

"Why didn't they write 'house' then?" said Jayne.

Ben grinned at her.

"Because it doesn't rhyme with 'chest', idiot."

Jayne kicked herself for being stupid, and Charlotte groaned.

"Oh no!" she said. "I hope it doesn't mean I've got to get into Cedric's *attic*! I can't bear it!"

"But you might have to," said Jayne.

"I don't think I can be Margery any more. Asking me to be nice to the Igmopong is like asking me to drink the washing-up water with all the bits floating in it."

"There's quite a lot of goodness in that," said Toby, grinning. "It's only the stuff that was on your dinner plate a bit earlier."

"And I suppose you've had some," said Charlotte, eyeing him sideways.

Toby grinned back, even wider, then Boff spoke.

"It's not in Cedric's house," he said. "Whatever it is."

The others turned to look at him.

"How can you possibly say that?" said Ben. But even as he said it, he knew it was too hasty. Boff didn't say much unless something really interested him. But when he did, his brain was so clear-thinking, it came up with the most extraordinary ideas. Ideas that the rest of them wouldn't think of in a week of Wednesdays. Before Ben could re-phrase his question, Charlotte did it for him.

"What makes you think that, Boff?"

Boff looked round at them.

"I'm pretty sure I'm right," he said apologetically. Even Boff realised that what he said had sounded high-handed. "I was just thinking this. If you wanted to hide something in a house, you wouldn't hide something else in the same house just to tell someone where the other thing was hidden. Do you see what I mean? I mean, there wouldn't be any point."

"Perhaps it was just an old treasure hunt game," said Ben, "And some of the clues were still left in the house."

"No," said Boff, firmly. "Let me try and explain a

different way. Remember the diagram was found in Deep Shadow Cottage? The diagram is leading someone to something hidden."

"A teddy bear," said Jayne.

"Well, yes, but whoever did the diagram knew where the teddy bear was hidden, and must have known there was a riddle inside it. So why bother to make someone find the teddy bear when the riddle could have been written on the diagram in the first place? No need for a diagram, either."

"It could still be a treasure hunt," said Jayne. "I think Ben's right. We've done a treasure hunt like that before, where one clue leads you to the next. It was one of our most exciting adventures."

"But that teddy bear must have been there for years," said Boff. "Cedric obviously knew nothing about it – especially as he fell for Charlotte's brilliant magic story. So I reckon the teddy bear's been there since before the Morgans moved in."

"When was that?" said Jayne.

"I remember the day," groaned Charlotte. "Vividly. I was only about four, but something told me Cedric was an idiot, even then."

"Do you see what I'm saying?" said Boff. "If it's been there that long, this isn't a treasure hunt. It's something more serious, but I can't quite get my mind around it. There's something else. . ."

"But if the teddy bear's clue isn't talking about Cedric's house, where is it talking about?" said Charlotte, who was feeling relieved, looking forward to not having to be Margery ever again.

"Well," said Boff. "It says 'Go to the top of *my nest*'. . ."

"But Teddy's nest is Cedric's house, isn't it?" said Ben.

"Yes," said Boff. "Sort of."

"So it *is* Cedric's house, then."

"No," said Boff. "No." Boff struggled to try to make his

meaning clear. "What I mean is. . . *the clue isn't from the teddy bear, it's from someone else.* The teddy bear was just somewhere to hide the clue – don't you see?"

"Yes, but. . ."

"So the person writing the clue is talking about where *he* lives—"

"Or she," put in Charlotte.

"Or she," said Boff. *"And where did Jayne and Toby find the diagram?"*

There was a two-second pause while Boff's words sank in, then everyone spoke at the same time.

"Deep Shadow Cottage!"

They all looked at one another and felt a new excitement stirring in their bones.

"How on earth are we going to get a look in the cottage?" said Charlotte.

"I'll get in," said Ben, the adventurous.

"I don't think we can break in," said Boff, trying to keep them calm.

"Well, we can't get in, then," said Ben. "We don't even know who owns it."

"We don't even know if anyone lives there," said Toby.

"However we do it, it all sounds brilliant fun," said Jayne. "But, Boff, I still don't understand. Why would someone who lived in Deep Shadow Cottage hide a teddy bear in someone *else's* house *years before* just to tell whoever finds it to go *back* to Deep Shadow Cottage to follow a clue that they could have given them at the cottage in the first place?"

It was a long sentence for Jayne, and Boff listened carefully and finally shook his head.

"I don't know," he said. "But I bet there's a really good reason, if only we could think of it."

CHAPTER SEVEN

Isaster-dang

Cedric and Doris had fully recovered from the flu, and Mrs Morgan set about finalising the plans for their midnight feast in the woods. She still didn't like the idea one bit, but a promise was a promise, and she had a bottomless capacity for spoiling her two darling children. Mrs Morgan believed that the more children were involved, the safer they would be. And more children meant more parents to supervise the woods and make sure everything was safe. So she allowed each member of Cedric's gang to invite one other friend. Cedric invited a small, quiet, spotty boy called Martin. Doris invited a nervous girl called Leila Slack who couldn't see in the dark, while Andy and Amanda both invited the same person, a cousin of theirs called Freddie. Freddie was very clever and they both admired him enormously.

"But you can invite someone *each*," said Doris.

"I know," said Amanda. "But we both like Freddie."

"Yeah," said Andy. "He's brillyunt."

"Well, I hope he can keep a secret," mumbled Cedric, who didn't like the idea of having someone 'brillyunt' at his precious midnight feast.

Mrs Morgan set up a meeting of all the parents involved early that evening.

"I do so wish I could be there to witness the little darlings enjoying their feast," Mrs Morgan sighed, when they were all gathered. "Cedric and Doris have been so *brave* during their illness. They're such sweet little children, and I want to give them just what they wanted as a reward."

"Do you think it's a good idea," interrupted Mr Wilson

70

(Andy and Amanda's father), "letting our children – at their tender age – loose in the woods at the dead of night? Anything might happen."

"What we don't want," said Martin's father, "is for there to be any danger to the children. Personally, I think it's foolhardy, but my boy is so brave about danger. . ."

"That's why it's so important not to breathe a word to anyone, not anyone," retorted Mrs Morgan. "We don't want any undesirable forces hearing about it. . ."

"I agree," said another voice. It was Leila's father, Colonel Slack, a little man with a military bearing. "It would be frightful if anything were to go belly-up. It's our responsibility to plan the whole thing with military precision. So I've drawn up some plans for everyone's approval, if Mr Morgan agrees. All right, Mr Morgan?"

Mr Morgan, a weedy little man, nodded. His only purpose in life was to obey commands, and he was always pleased if someone – it didn't matter who – told him what to do.

In the absence of any challenge, Colonel Slack handed round sheets of paper to the group and suggested that they move across the road to the woods and walk it through before dark.

The Naitabals had no idea who owned Gray's Wood, even though they had always used it as if it were their own. And they had no idea if that owner also owned the cottage.

The first person they thought of asking, of course, was Mr Elliott. But with Mr Elliott out working again until dusk, there was no quick answer. They asked every parent and adult friend available, but none of them knew who owned Gray's Wood either. While the Naitabals looked forward anxiously for Mr Elliott to come back from work, they decided to continue keeping watch on the cottage. It was an outside chance, but they hoped they might be lucky and see something or someone who might help them.

Boff and Ben volunteered to go first, after tea. They climbed a tree overlooking Deep Shadow Cottage, where they had a good view without being visible themselves. Jayne and Toby stayed behind in the Naitabal hut and watched as Charlotte started to put the teddy bear back together again.

The party of Igmopong parents set off with the colonel in the lead, heading along the paths through the trees. The pace of his leadership was brisk, and by the time they arrived at Deep Shadow Cottage, half of the followers were puffing and blowing.

He turned to address the ragged group only ten metres from the tree in which Boff and Ben were hiding. The two Naitabals recognised the Igmopong parents, Mr Morgan and Mr and Mrs Wilson, but the other adults were strangers. They heard every syllable of the leader's high-pitched voice.

"Now the first essential of any operation of this sort," Colonel Slack began, "is to have a focal meeting place. A headquarters, as it were. Like any other wood, this whole area is just one tree after another, and unless you're a woodpecker, they all look the same. So it's no good saying we'll gather at such-and-such a tree because half of us won't find it, and the other half'll go to the wrong tree and think they're at the right tree." He let out a slow chuckle, then turned and swept his arm towards the cottage.

"Now, there's only one landmark in the entire jungle on this side of the river, and this is it. Deep Shadow Cottage. Odd name, but there it is on the gate. So we'll all come here in the first instance with the children and we'll lead off from here."

Ben and Boff exchanged glances. At first they had thought the party was something to do with the cottage, but now they began to realise it was something else.

"We'll also meet back here at the end when the little

blighters' bellies are full of tuck. Then we'll go and fetch them out. We'll also meet back here before time's up if I give three sharp blasts on my whistle. Like this."

He took a silver whistle from his top pocket and gave it three hearty lungfuls that had everyone covering their ears.

"Got all that?"

They all said, yes, they had got all that.

"So the plan is this," the colonel continued in his strident voice, "I've already obtained permission from the landowner, Mr Leonard. . ."

Ben and Boff exchanged glances again, eyebrows raised.

". . .He's kindly agreed that we can put a lamp at each corner of the wall round the cottage so we can see the thing in the dark. You won't miss it, I can assure you. It'll be like a lighthouse.

"At 2300 hours on Friday we gather here and I will hand out bundles of white linen strips. We will then set out to lay a trail by tying white strips to every third or fourth tree. In the deepest, thickest part of the wood (to make it more exciting for the young blisters), we'll tie a small circle of strips, one on every tree. Those of you bringing up the rear will be carrying the hampers, and they'll be placed in the middle of the circle. We'll all clear out by following the white trail back to headquarters here. Then you'll all retreat to your key positions round the perimeter of the wood to guard against unwelcome intruders. The children will be brought over at exactly a quarter to twelve and we'll release them from here. They'll follow the trail with a torch, find the food at around midnight, consume it, and then return along the marked trail to me here at the cottage. Finally, I'll give three blasts on the whistle, which is your signal to come and collect your offspring.

"Does everyone agree that this gives adequate security?" asked the colonel.

There was a muffled chorus of assent, and then the colonel

started to lead them off along one of the paths.

"Now if you look at the map I've given you, this path leads to the perimeter point at. . ." His voice faded into the trees.

Up in their hiding place, Ben and Boff were staring at each other, grinning from ear to ear.

In the Naitabal hut, Charlotte picked up the teddy bear and started pummelling its stuffing back into place so she could sew up its wound. It was when she was feeling its legs that she turned to Jayne and Toby.

"Hey!" she said. "There's something else in here! I was so excited when I found the note I didn't even *think* there might be anything else."

"What sort of thing is it?" said Jayne.

"It feels solid, like wood or metal. Hang on."

Charlotte sat on the floor and used Ben's penknife again to unpick a few more stitches in the teddy bear's back. With the larger hole, her fingers could explore every millimetre of stuffing.

"There's nothing else in his tummy," she said. "And nothing in his arms. Now for the legs." Her fingers probed deeper and deeper until she let out a little cry.

"Definitely something here!" she squealed.

She changed the angle of her hand, pushed in two fingers instead of one, and drew out something with bits of stuffing still attached to it.

"It's a key!" she said. "Look!" She held it up in triumph. Then her fingers groped another leg, and seconds later produced another key. She laid the pair on the floor, and the three of them gazed in wonder.

"Wow!" said Jayne. "Well done, Charlotte! Good job you looked!"

Charlotte satisfied herself that there was nothing but stuffing left inside the bear, then arranged it evenly inside. She began the job of sewing it together neatly again with the brown cotton she'd fetched from her house. While she was doing it, they discussed the keys.

"I wonder if these are our passport to the cottage?" said Toby.

"They don't look big enough to me for front door keys," said Charlotte. "That one looks like it opens a cupboard or perhaps an internal door, but not a front door."

"The other one could be a back door key," said Toby, hopefully.

"We can try," said Jayne.

But that was their last piece of good news before disaster struck.

Disaster struck in the middle of the evening, when it was nearing the end of Boff and Ben's turn to keep an eye on the cottage. The sounds of hammers banging that echoed through the wood from the east didn't sound like disaster. Ben and Boff thought nothing of it. It sounded like one of their neighbours fixing a fence, or someone putting up a garden shed. It still didn't feel like disaster when they heard footsteps running towards them through the wood. When they saw that the running feet belonged to Toby and Jayne and Charlotte, they thought something might be wrong, but not *that* wrong.

The three breathless bodies that arrived at the base of their tree made no attempt at a quiet, secretive approach. They'd broken all the rules and they stood looking up with pale and frightened faces.

"Boff! Ben! Come down!"

Now they knew something was wrong. Badly wrong.

"What is it?"

They dropped down as quickly as they could, frowns creasing their foreheads. No one else was about. No one had followed them. Toby gave out the terrible news.

"Gray's Wood is up for sale!" he said. He tried to hold

back a sob in his voice, but didn't succeed.

"What!!"

"They've just put up the signs. It says it's to be sold for *building development!*"

It was the worst possible news they could ever have imagined. The woods up for sale was one thing – in a way, it didn't matter. If the new owner didn't change anything, what was the difference? But the woods being sold for building. . . It was as if someone had taken a sledgehammer to the Naitabals themselves.

Gray's Wood, which lay opposite Boff's and Charlotte's and Cedric's and Mr Elliott's houses, was a hundred and sixty acres in total. It had been used by the Naitabals so often for their games and for hiding from the Igmopong, that in their minds it had really become part of their own Naitabal Territory. They might never run along its tracks in Naitabal battledress again, stalking each other in silence, or yelling at the tops of their blood-curdling voices, or chasing the Igmopong. The thought was almost more than they could bear. The thought that houses might be built on it was a tragedy.

They loved its long grassy patches, its thick tangles of bramble, its blackberries in the summer, its hazelnuts in the autumn. They loved its trees, tall and old and majestic. Perfect for climbing, hiding in and making secret camps. They loved the humorous cackle of the green woodpeckers. They loved watching the zig-zag of the nuthatches and tree creepers climbing the tree trunks, the beautiful songs of the blackbirds and thrushes, the high sweet trill of the wren and the liquid warble of the robin. Life without Gray's Wood would be like death itself.

It wasn't as if they trespassed in the wood. It was private property, but the unknown owner had never sealed it off, and the public had enjoyed free access for many years. In return, they treated it with respect and didn't disturb the wildlife.

Mournfully, all five Naitabals walked back to the tree-house to discuss the tragic news. It threw a shadow over everything: the discovery of Cedric's secret midnight feast, the discovery of the name of the man who owned Gray's Wood, the teddy bear's message, and even the fact that Charlotte had found two keys that might give them access to Deep Shadow Cottage.

"It's all too much of a coincidence," said Boff suddenly. "Do you realise what's happened in just nine or ten days?"

In the safety and comfort of the tree-house, the other Naitabals watched him and listened.

"One. Jayne sees a face at the window of the cottage for the first time ever. Two. Toby finds a diagram in the rubbish at the cottage. Three. Charlotte finds a teddy bear, hidden in Cedric's house for at least six years. Four. The woods and the cottage go on sale. Is that all too much coincidence, or what? I think there's a connection running right through all of it."

"I see what you mean," said Ben. "It's as if there's something special going on, isn't it?"

None of them could guess what the 'something special' was, but it did mean that they had work to do. The worst part of the news was the sale of the woods, and the Naitabals knew they would never rest until they had saved them from being felled and built on. It was truly horrible.

The following morning, they would split up into teams. Boff would go to the estate agents on his own – their name was displayed on the sale boards for the woods – to try to find out the address of the owner. They knew his name was Mr Leonard because Boff and Ben had overheard the Igmopong fathers say so. Jayne and Charlotte would go to the cottage, make absolutely sure no one was looking, and try the keys in the front and back doors. If one key fitted, they would go inside and see if the second key fitted an internal door or cupboard. They wouldn't explore, but would lock up again and retreat, climb the tree and stay on watch. Ben and Toby would go to the local council offices and see if any planning permission had been granted for building on the woodland area.

Minutes later, the Naitabal hut was securely locked and deserted. They all needed a good night's sleep.

CHAPTER EIGHT

Ark-dang Adows-shong

Mrs Josie Fern, an attractive woman in her early thirties, sat at her breakfast table, eating toast and sipping coffee. The postman had just been and she quickly rifled through the half dozen envelopes that had been pushed through her door. Her dog, a spoilt white poodle, had reached them first, so several had a pattern of needle-thin teeth marks in their edges. She put aside the savaged electricity bill in disgust, followed by the punctured final demand for the telephone, and threw three gnawed mailshots straight into the bin. The last letter, from a firm of solicitors, made her suddenly sit up straight in her chair. She finished the ripping-open that the dog had started, and read the contents with interest.

Dear Mrs Fern,
This is to inform you that your ex-husband, Derek D Fern, died in hospital on Tuesday last following a series of heart attacks, and was cremated two days later.
He died penniless. His will (copy enclosed) leaves his few possessions to charity. Please, therefore, do not write to us again requesting his whereabouts. His file is now closed.
Yours sincerely, etc etc.

Mrs Fern flipped the sheet over and read the one underneath, headed 'Last Will and Testament of Derek Daniel Fern.' She skimmed over the legal nonsense and read the important part.

I leave any cash left over from my pension, along with

*what few chattels I possess, to the British Heart Foundation.
To my ex-wife Josie Fern, I say good riddance. You don't
deserve a penny, and you don't get one.*
Signed, Derek D Fern.

Mrs Fern threw the letter on to the table in disgust, where it
landed across the butter dish. She picked up her directory
and looked up 'Hospitals'. She dialled the first number.

"Hello, is that the Queen Elizabeth Hospital? My name is
Josie Fern. My husband died there last Tuesday. His things
should have been sent home, but they haven't arrived, and I
wondered what address they were sent to? We'd moved
recently, you see, and he was rather forgetful, and I'm
wondering if he gave you an old address by mistake?"

There was a pause at the other end while enquiries were
made.

"I'm sorry," said the receptionist eventually. "We have no
record of anyone of that name here."

"Oh, silly me, I've rung the wrong hospital. Goodbye."

Mrs Fern rang several more hospitals and said exactly the
same words to each of them. They assured her that her
husband had not died there, and that she must have made a
mistake. At last she found the hospital she wanted.

"Hello, is that the Markyate Hospital? My name is Josie
Fern. My husband died there last Tuesday. His things
should have been sent home, but they haven't arrived, and I
wondered what address they were sent to? We'd moved
recently, you see, and he was rather forgetful, and I'm
wondering if he gave you an old address by mistake?"

The voice at the other end, a young, fresh voice, said that it
would just check for her.

"Hello?" said the voice. "The address we've got is Deep
Shadow Cottage, Gray's Wood. But his clothes were
collected, not sent."

"Who collected them?"

"A Mr Leonard?"

"Ah. That explains it. I'll deal with it, thank you. Goodbye." Mrs Fern slammed down the receiver and added, "Stupid young girl! Fancy giving out personal information to any stranger who happens to ring up! They'll never learn." A smile crept round the thick red line of her lips, as she wrote 'Deep Shadow Cottage' and 'Mr Leonard' on the back of the solicitor's letter.

"Well," she said aloud. "Deep Shadow Cottage."

The poodle pricked up its ears, searching for the word 'walk', but it wasn't there.

"Deep Shadow Cottage," she repeated. "Gray's Wood. So that's where you've been skulking these last seven years, you horrible little man."

Boff took a deep breath and pushed open the door of the estate agent that bore the legend Leeward, Windward and Breeze. A youngish man in a suit was sitting at a desk talking to a customer. Another, older, man was sitting at a desk. He had one finger on a list in front of him and had just picked up the telephone. Seeing Boff, he put it down again.

"Hello, young sir. What can I do for you?"

"Hello," said Boff.

"Take a seat."

"Thank you." Boff sat down. "I was wondering if it's possible to tell me the name of the owner of Gray's Wood that's just come on the market?"

"Interested in buying it, eh?" the man joked.

"No. I'd like to talk to him."

"That's confidential information, I'm afraid, young sir. We never give out client details, buyers or sellers."

"How can I talk to him, then?"

"If you write him a letter, I'll make sure he gets it. Then, if he wants to talk to you, he'll contact you direct. How's that?"

"Thank you," said Boff. "That seems fine. By the way, what's the asking price?"

"Thinking of saving up, are you?"

Boff gave a ghost of a smile.

"Well, it's open to offers," the man continued. "If it's wanted for building, then it could fetch a few million or more. If someone wants it for the cottage, or no one can get building permission, it might go for a fraction of that."

"I see. Does that mean that no one has given permission for building yet?"

"That's right. A builder might buy it on spec and hope to get planning permission in the future if he can't get it now. It could be built on next year, or in thirty years. Who knows?"

Boff stood up.

"Thank you very much for your help."

"Don't mention it."

"I'll bring in a letter for you to give to the owner." They shook hands and Boff added, "Would it be possible to have a set of the particulars for the property?"

As the estate agent rummaged in a filing cabinet, Boff stood aside to allow an attractive woman to come in the door carrying a white poodle. She approached a woman who had just returned to a third desk and spoke in a low breathy voice.

"Hello. My name's Josie Fern. I'm looking for a secluded house, preferably with land and plenty of trees. Do you have anything like that?"

"Well, er. . ."

"Up to a million pounds," she added, smiling sweetly.

The first man had found Boff's sheets and turned his head to look at the newcomer.

"Can I help?" he said, dismissing his assistant with a nod. He handed the particulars to Boff brusquely without even looking at him again, and pulled out another set for the woman.

Boff stood pretending to read while the conversation continued.

"We have this *very* secluded cottage with a hundred and sixty acres of mature English woodland. . ."

"That sounds nice," said the woman, taking the sheets. "Where is it, exactly?"

"It's just down the road from here, known as Gray's Wood."

"Who is selling?"

"Ah. That's confidential."

"Does anyone live there at the moment?"

"No. Sadly, the tenant died. That's the reason for the sale, now it's empty."

"And who was the tenant? Anyone I might have known?"

The estate agent coughed.

"I'm afraid the vendor has asked for that to be kept confidential, too. In fact, we don't know who the tenant was. Not that it matters. The cottage and the wood are for sale with vacant possession. We've put the boards up, but there's one locked door that needs the locksmith on it before we can officially show anyone round. . ."

"Oh, but surely, as I'm in the area *now*. . . ?" the woman simpered.

Boff had heard enough. He opened the door quietly, still pretending to read, and slipped away.

Jayne and Charlotte reached Deep Shadow Cottage without being followed by the Igmopong, who were strangely and unusually quiet. They slipped in through the gate after double checking that no one was around, then Charlotte's nervous fingers produced the two keys from her jeans pocket and tried the larger one in the lock in the front door. It was far too small and just rattled around in the lock.

"No good," Charlotte whispered. "Let's try the back."

They crept round behind the wall, keeping low in case anyone was watching from a distance. The keyhole in the back door looked more promising, and Charlotte inserted the key and gave it a twist. It went in tidily, and there was a sweet click as it turned all the way round.

"That's it!" hissed Charlotte. She was so excited she could hardly get the key out again.

"Shall we go in?" said Jayne, excited too.

"Aren't we trespassing or burgling or something?"

"We're not breaking and entering this time," said Jayne. "Not like Ben and Toby and Cedric's room. We've got a key."

"It's still entering," said Charlotte. "It must still be half a crime."

"Oh, come on. We're here. The door's open. It's what we agreed."

Against her better judgment, Charlotte was weakening.

"Anyway," Jayne persisted, "loads of people are going to come and look at it to see if they want to buy it. It's not as if we're doing any harm."

"I know – we're just seeing if we can find out where the other key fits."

"That's it."

"Then we can come back with the others and try and solve the teddy bear riddle."

"Yes. That sounds good."

Jayne turned the door handle and they slipped quietly inside. Charlotte locked the door behind them. They found themselves in a small old-fashioned kitchen, the walls showing the shapes of the brickwork directly underneath thick layers of green glossy paint on the lower half and yellow up above. There was a hand water-pump near the sink. Jayne gave it a push and caused a deep gurgle in the earth which made them both jump.

"Don't touch anything else!" pleaded Charlotte. "You've

already frightened me half to death!"

They went quickly round the little house looking for locked doors, but couldn't find one until they returned to the kitchen and tried all the cupboards. One cupboard door wouldn't open, but it had a keyhole, and Charlotte produced the other key from her pocket and tried it in the lock. It turned, and the door was free.

The two exchanged excited glances as the door swung open to reveal not a cupboard, but steps leading down to a basement or cellar.

"We don't go any further," said Charlotte, closing the door. "We promised the others we wouldn't do any exploring without them."

"Okay," said Jayne. "We did promise. And we've checked *both* keys, so now we know where they fit."

"And it proves Boff was right about the riddle," said Charlotte. "It proves it's this house, not Cedric's, otherwise the keys wouldn't fit."

"That's right."

Suddenly the girls froze as if someone had thrown an icy blanket around them. Outside the front door they had picked up the unmistakable sound of footsteps and voices approaching.

"Oh no!" squealed Jayne in a whisper. "What shall we do?"

There was no time to unlock the back door, escape and lock it again, especially as there was a risk they'd be seen leaving the cottage.

"Quick! Down here!" hissed Charlotte, sounding desperate. She flung open the door to the cellar and thrust Jayne in front of her down the steps. She followed and turned to lock the door from the inside. There were no bolts to make a thorough job of it, so anyone with a key could get in and find them. They could only hope that no one else had a key, or that the visitors would not want to come down.

85

It was nearly completely dark in the cellar, except for patches of light that strayed through a very dirty horizontal narrow window high up in one wall.

There was lots of equipment and machinery in the cellar, and they quickly chose good hiding places in case anyone came down.

They could hear the sounds of a key being turned in the front door, and voices – a man and a woman, and a small dog yapping.

"This is it," said the man.

"It's quite tidy," said the woman. "But you're right. It is in need of decoration and a certain amount of cleaning."

"It needs some modernisation, too. As you'll see in the kitchen, water still has to be pumped from the underground reservoir."

"What do you know about the owner. Why is he selling?"

"He's selling because he needs the money for retirement, I believe. The tenant died very recently, as I told you, and that's given him the opportunity to sell. I don't think he wanted to sell while the tenant was still living here."

"I see most of the tenant's belongings are still here. . ."

The voices were in the kitchen now. Suddenly the handle of the cellar door rattled and made the girls' hearts jump.

"That's the cellar," said the man. "I'm afraid we don't have a key for that at present. As I said, as soon as the locksmith has opened it we can put the house officially on the market. You're privileged, you see."

The voices receded up the stairs, and Jayne and Charlotte exchanged glances in the near-darkness from behind their pieces of equipment.

Charlotte examined her surroundings more closely and realised, as her eyes grew accustomed to the poor light, that she was hiding behind a big, colour photocopier. It was covered in a transparent plastic sheet, thick with dust. When she stood up and lifted the corner she could see the selection buttons, and big trays sticking out to catch the copied sheets, like the ones in photocopy shops. The machine itself looked clean and modern, and very expensive. She found herself wondering why anyone would keep such a thing in their cellar. Perhaps the tenant was running a business. It was strange that no one had ever seen him, though, she thought to herself.

Jayne was doing the same in her own hiding place. Hers was a huge metal cabinet with a dangerous-looking electric guillotine on top, rather dusty. It was the sort of guillotine that could cut through a ream of paper like butter. She'd seen one used once when her father had taken her to a printing company to pick up some work.

Jayne, too, wondered why such a big machine would be in someone's cellar. Especially when it was someone that no one ever saw.

Presently the voices came down the stairs again and made their way to the front door.

"Would it be all right to come back on my own and take a closer look at everything?" the woman's voice said sweetly.

"Well, we don't normally let people here on their own, I'm afraid. . ."

"Well, you could come with me and make sure I didn't run away with any furniture. . ." the woman giggled.

The voices receded as the key turned in the lock. Presently a vehicle started, and the faint purr of its engine dissolved into the silence of the wood.

Up in the Naitabal hut, Ben and Toby had returned from the council offices with the same story that Boff had learned from the estate agent. No planning permission had been granted for building in the woods, and no application had been received.

Boff was writing a letter to Mr Leonard, care of the estate agent.

87

*

In the estate agent's car, the lady with the poodle was giving sweet smiles and leaning towards the man as he drove, asking for the twentieth time if it was possible for her to borrow the key and have a look around the cottage more thoroughly by herself.

The man, worn down by her charm and her bright smile, said that, yes, he thought it might be possible if he talked to the owner.

Jayne and Charlotte came out of their hiding places, much relieved, and Charlotte started looking for a light switch. She found it at the top of the stairs, and the little cellar flooded with light.

"Have you seen this?" she said, pointing to the colour photocopier.

"Wow!" said Jayne. "And look at mine. I was hiding behind a guillotine."

"I wonder why someone would want all this stuff down in the cellar," Charlotte continued. She idly raised the lid of the photocopier, and caught her breath so suddenly, she almost choked.

"Jayne, look!" she gurgled.

Jayne looked. And screamed.

CHAPTER NINE

Claustrophobia

Charlotte and Jayne couldn't believe what they were looking at. Lying on the flat bed of the photocopier was a frame of plastic and glass. And mounted on the glass were six £50 notes. Charlotte carefully lifted the frame off and discovered that it had been made so precisely that it only fitted back on the photocopier bed in one position.

"He's been photocopying £50 notes!" said Charlotte. "In colour!"

"Look!" said Jayne. She was pointing at another frame propped against the wall near the photocopier, another frame with six £50 notes in it. She tried the frame on the flat bed, but it only fitted one way. "These are mounted the other way over," said Jayne.

"I see!" said Charlotte. "Look! Your frame does the fronts, and this frame does the backs!"

"Charlotte!" said Jayne. "You know what this means, don't you? It means the man who lived here was a forger!"

Charlotte wrinkled her nose.

"But you can't forge £50 notes with a *photocopier*!" she said. "They wouldn't fool anyone for a second!"

"Well, why would anyone do it, then?"

"I don't know," said Charlotte, dropping the first frame back into place and closing the lid. "Come on. All I know is we've got to get out of here before anyone else comes. Let's get back and tell the others what we've found!"

Jayne replaced her frame where she had found it, then they climbed the little wooden steps. Charlotte unlocked the door. She made doubly sure she'd locked it properly, then she and Jayne crept out of the back door, making certain that that was properly locked as well. Before emerging from the gate they checked that no one was around. Finding it clear, they ran back to the Naitabal hut as fast as their legs would take them.

When everyone had caught up with everyone else's news, the five Naitabals discussed the strange things that Jayne and Charlotte had found at Deep Shadow Cottage.

"We're really sorry we went into the cellar when we weren't supposed to," Charlotte apologised, "but it was our only escape route. The man and woman would have seen us if we'd gone out the back door again."

"Any of us would have done the same," said Ben.

"You bet," said Toby, grinning. "I wish I'd been there."

"So what we seem to have," said Boff, "is a teddy bear with two keys inside. One leads you into the cottage, and the other into the cellar. So the second key has nothing to do with the teddy bear's message, because that tells you to go to the highest part of the house. But the key takes you to the lowest part. And in the lowest part you find very modern technology with a very clear method of copying £50 notes which, as Charlotte says – and we all agree – wouldn't fool anyone for more than five seconds." Boff's glasses glinted in the mid-morning sun as he looked round at them all. "There's something very peculiar going on here," he concluded. Then he added, rather disappointingly, "And I haven't the faintest idea what it is."

"Let's hope your letter's delivered to Mr Leonard nice and quickly," said Ben. "Perhaps he can tell us something about the mystery man who lived there."

Boff's letter was delivered promptly in person by the estate agent to Mr Leonard, the owner of the wood. Mr Leonard telephoned Boff early that same afternoon. He sounded pleasant, and he invited all five Naitabals to come and see him at his house, which was a short walk away on the outskirts of the village.

Mr Leonard was a kindly man, it turned out. He was grey-haired and bony, close to retirement, and he lived on his own in a very modest terraced house. He greeted the five Naitabals with warmth and humour, showed them into his small sitting-room, and listened politely to what they had to say.

"Please, Mr Leonard," Ben began, "we don't mean to bother you, but we heard that you're going to sell Gray's Wood so they can cut all the trees down and build houses on it. Is it really true?" There was a little lump lurking in Ben's throat, but he tried his best to hide it.

Mr Leonard smiled as he looked round at the five anxious faces.

"I think we need to discuss this calmly over a nice drink and a biscuit, don't you?" he said.

He served them with hot drinks and cool bars of chocolate, and when they were all settled again, he gave them his answer.

"I'm afraid it is true," he said. "Up to a point, anyway. It's the last thing I would want to happen to Gray's Wood, too, but I don't see how I can stop it."

"Can't you stop it by not selling it?" pleaded Charlotte, trying very hard not to sound impolite. She knew it was a rude thing to say, but she felt she had to say it. If she didn't say it, she wouldn't know the answer.

"I wish I could," said Mr Leonard. "But Life's not as straightforward as that – unless you're *very* lucky." He sighed. "I'm coming up to retirement now and, frankly, it's not too soon. I feel so tired these days I can hardly work a few hours on the trot without having a sleep for a couple more. And then the day's half gone and I've nothing much to show for it. But I haven't saved for my retirement – I've never had enough spare cash for it. All I've got is Gray's Wood and the old cottage there. I rent this house, see, I don't own it. Now, when I stop working I won't have any income at all – except what the miserly old government will give me for forty-nine years work, and I won't be able to live on it, not with renting a house as well."

"Why don't you live in the house in the woods?" said Jayne. It came out sounding like a rude question as well, not like she meant it at all, but it was too late now. "I'm sorry, I didn't mean. . ."

"That's all right, young lady," Mr Leonard smiled on her kindly. "I suffer from claustrophobia, that's the trouble. I couldn't live in a wood to save my life, all those dark trees around me. And I can see from the expressions on all your faces that you'd all *love* to live in a wood!"

"You bet!"

"Yes, please!"

"Well, I just can't. It's a great pity, it sounds daft, but there it is. Perhaps it was my mother reading Little Red Riding Hood and making me scared of the wolf.

"I only inherited the wood seven years ago, so if I'd never been given it, I wouldn't have had money to retire on anyway, and that would have been that. I can tell you, I wasn't looking forward to being a burden to the State and having to go cap in hand to the Social Security to get a few extra pounds. My pride doesn't like it. But I *was* given the wood, see. Well – I can't live in it and if I don't sell it I'm back to square one – no money to live on and a house to rent. So what else can I do but sell it?"

"But why do you have to sell it to someone who wants to clear it and build houses on it?" asked Boff.

Mr Leonard shrugged.

"I may not have any choice. It's only been on the market for two days so far but the only people who are likely to be interested in it are the building companies. Although I did see one lady and a yappy poodle who came round interested in buying it. She wants a closer look, but I don't know if she's serious. She asked plenty of questions, though. Of course, builders would have to get permission from the local council, the planning department and so on. But a lot of these builders try to buy stuff cheap. Then they just wait for donkey's years until they can get planning permission, or until they can bribe a few people on the council."

"That's really horrible," said Boff, and the others agreed.

"I'm not greedy," said Mr Leonard, making it very clear. "I could hold out for millions of pounds for that land, or more if I wanted to, if two builders were fighting over it. But if I show a weakness – if they think I've got to sell quickly – they'll be crafty. They'll get together and knock the price down low and then share it between them. No, I'm not greedy, but I *want* whoever buys it to keep it as a wood forever. It's called putting it in trust. Then you know that no greedy person in the future's going to be buying it just to sell it to a builder later on at a big profit.

"The problem is, I can't find anyone who wants it just as a wood. I'd happily take two hundred thousand pounds if that would keep me looked after for the rest of my days, but no one wants to pay two hundred thousand just to keep it as a wood. I'd take two hundred thousand if it was guaranteed to be kept as a wood for ever. Even then, someone might buy it for two hundred thousand and *say* they'll keep it as a wood, and then sell it to the builders for two million. Horrible, isn't it?"

The Naitabals had rarely listened to such a long explanation in their lives before, but now they all understood the situation that Mr Leonard found himself in. He only needed enough money to invest to give himself a comfortable income for his retirement, but no one wanted to buy the wood and keep it just as a wood. There'd always be a danger that someone would buy it just to make a profit –

someone who didn't care about the green woodpeckers and the thousands of species that depended on the oak trees.

"I wish we could buy it," said Jayne. "I wish we had forty thousand pounds each so that we could buy it and call it the Naitabal Trust and keep it as a wood for ever."

"Yes," said Ben. "I wish we were old enough to have saved up enough money to buy it ourselves. Then it would *never* be built on."

"I don't know how long I can hold out," said Mr Leonard, shaking his head. "I retire in five weeks time, and it won't be long after that when I run out of money. And I can't really sell it until a certain something happens, either. But I've put it on the market straight away to get ahead of the game. I haven't even had time to go and clean it, and now there's no one living there it ought to be boarded up in case anyone breaks in. Two of the rooms need decorating, so I'm told, and I've no money to pay anyone to do anything. I can't stay in the woods for more than an hour myself, with my claustrophobia, not that I've got the time. It's a desperate situation, kids, it's a sad one, and no mistake. *You* don't think I'm being greedy or unreasonable, do you? I wouldn't want you to think that."

"Of course we don't," said Ben. "We understand now."

"We'll see if we can do anything to help," said Charlotte.

"Yes," said Jayne. "Couldn't we clean and decorate it for you?"

But Boff's incisive brain had picked up a phrase of Mr Leonard's and latched on to it, and before Mr Leonard could consider Jayne's offer, Boff jumped in.

"What did you mean when you said you couldn't sell it until a certain something happened?" he said.

Mr Leonard looked at Boff keenly.

"You lot don't miss much, do you?" he said with a twinkle in his eye. "It's a long story, but can I trust you to keep a secret?"

"Of course you can!" said Charlotte. "We're – we're Naitabals, and Naitabals *never* give away secrets."

"Naitabals, eh? And what are Naitabals when they're at home?"

Between them, Charlotte and the others explained to Mr Leonard everything about their subculture. They explained about the tree-house that Mr Elliott had built for them, and how they had their own language, their own rules, their own Naitabal Morse code, and their own lots of other things. Some of them were secret so, of course, they couldn't tell him about those. They told him how they had solved some mysteries, and how he could talk to a Miss Coates if he wanted to, a neighbour of theirs, to check if they could keep a secret.

Mr Leonard laughed when they had finished.

"I wish I'd been in a gang like yours when I was your age," he said. "Not that I would have been as bright as you lot."

He stood up.

"Well, how about I top up your teacups, and then I'll tell you *my* secret if you'll promise not to tell *anyone* else, and I mean *anyone*."

"We promise. And a Naitabal promise is a *real* promise."

"I said it was a long story, but it's not," Mr Leonard began. "Not really. It started about twenty years ago, long before you were born. It was freezing winter, the coldest we'd had for years, and the river in Gray's Wood was frozen over in places. I was taking my dog for a walk along the bank (I don't mind the open part of the wood near the river – in the winter, when the trees are bare). I noticed that a man was ice-skating on the river a short way away. I thought it was a stupid thing to do. The river was frozen over, yes, but you could see it was thin in places, and it needs to be a few inches thick to be safe. Anyway, seconds later there was a crack and the skater disappeared into the icy water.

95

"Now I was downstream from him, and my first thought was he'd be swept along by the current. It was usually quite a slow current and there'd been no rain or deep snow for weeks, so it was probably slow that day. And somehow my mind worked like a computer and *I worked out what route the water would take* – I'd stood and gazed at the river often enough when it wasn't frozen, so perhaps my brain already knew how the water went. So I found a great big log by the river bank, almost as big as I could move, and I rolled it end over end into the river so it would fall hard and break the ice in the place I wanted. And would you believe it, the log crashed in, made a terrific splash of water and jagged lumps of ice, and the skater popped out of the hole like magic! I reached down and grabbed him, hauled him out with the dog barking because he thought I'd thrown a big bone for him, and then excited because I'd found him a plaything in the river."

Mr Leonard chuckled.

"Well, the man was shocked and freezing cold, so I gave him my coat and hat and got him walking back to my little house here. I'd saved his life, see." Mr Leonard stopped as tears welled in his eyes. "He'd have drowned for sure if I hadn't made that hole in the right place. I might even have killed him by dropping the log on him, but I didn't. I saved him.

"Well, he was a businessman, had his own big joinery business, I mean, and wanted to give me rewards and everything, but I said I only did what anyone would have done, so I didn't take anything, although he sent me a big hamper every Christmas. And then, about seven years ago he gave me the wood and the cottage. *Gave them to me.* Wouldn't take no for an answer. Said it was a fraction of what he owned, he wouldn't miss it, made the deeds out in my name, and all I had to do was sign a few bits of paper, and they were mine."

Mr Leonard paused again, took a tissue from the box next to his chair and blew his nose.

"That's better. Well. There were two conditions, but he only said them afterwards, when I'd already signed, so they weren't strictly legal or anything."

"What were they?" said Boff.

"Well, the first was that he had free use of the cottage for the rest of his life – to live in, I mean. He was nearly seventy by then, so it didn't matter too much, and anyway I wasn't going to live there with my claustrophobia."

"Was the man who lived in the cottage *the man who gave it to you*, then?" said Charlotte, shocked.

"That's right, young miss. But *that's a secret*. You don't tell that to anyone – *or that I saved his life, or that he gave me the wood*. Those are the secrets."

"We'll never tell anyone," said Boff. "We're the only five people who'll know. But what was the second condition?"

"Very strange, this one. He asked that I didn't sell the cottage until I was given the other half of a piece of paper he gave me. I've got it locked away. He can't stop me selling, of course, because everything's legally mine, but he knew I was a man of my word, and I won't sell until I get that other half piece of paper. Goodness knows where it'll come from, but I only hope it comes soon."

"Can we see the paper, Mr Leonard?" asked Jayne sweetly.

"Of course you can. I'll get it."

Mr Leonard disappeared and came back half a minute later holding a piece of blue notepaper.

"It's the left-hand side of a sheet, torn down the middle," he said, showing it to them. Just a list of words in a column that don't make any sense."

P.S., Don't, anyone, the, that, burnt, the, were, from, loose, nice, in, I, the, ones, you!

The Naitabals all studied the sheet, but could make no sense of it. But at least they knew what the missing half might look like.

"Has he died now?" asked Ben. "Is that what's happened?"

Even as Mr Leonard answered, Boff was whispering under his breath to himself, "*That's what happened, that's what made everything start happening. . .*"

"Yes," Mr Leonard was answering, "he died a week ago in hospital. Had a mild heart attack at the cottage and put all his affairs in order, cycled – yes, cycled – to the hospital and had another heart attack the next day and died."

"Perhaps this piece of paper's with his will?" said Boff.

"No. The will's been read. And that's the weird bit."

"What?"

"Well, his will says he died penniless." Mr Leonard took up his tissue again as his voice started to break. "*It means he gave me everything he had.* If I'd have known I wouldn't have taken it, but he told me it was a fraction, just a fraction. *And it was everything!*"

The Naitabals looked on helplessly as Mr Leonard wiped his eyes and gave his nose another blast into a new tissue.

"Don't upset yourself, Mr Leonard," said Charlotte gently. "You saved his life. He wanted you to have it."

Toby had been quiet up till now, but it was Toby who asked the question that the others were dying to ask, and that Jayne had already asked, but they'd forgotten.

"Mr Leonard," he said. "Will you let us clean and decorate the cottage for you?"

Mr Leonard smiled gratefully.

"Would you?" he said. "Would you really? It'd be a great weight off my mind."

"Of course we will," said Charlotte. "Naitabals can do anything."

"And you never know," said Jayne, "we might find the other half of that piece of paper – if you don't mind us looking," she added hastily.

"You look all you want," said Mr Leonard. He knew she meant well – they seemed a great bunch of kids. But he couldn't see that there was anything they could do in *that* strange department.

But that, of course, was where Mr Leonard was wrong.

CHAPTER TEN

In Limb, O Hollow Chest

"What I don't understand," said Charlotte as they were walking home, "is how this Mr Penniless thought he could get away with forging £50 notes on a photocopier. It just doesn't make any sense at all, does it?"

"No," said Ben. "Fancy giving the wood and the cottage away and then having to be a criminal to live."

They were approaching Naitabal territory now, and kept their voices low, ready to switch to Naitabal language if anyone came in sight.

"There's more to it than that," said Boff, "I'm certain. There's the teddy bear and there's the rhyming clue, and there's this half a piece of paper. It's weird that he's been asked not to sell until someone gives him the other half."

"Weird isn't the word," said Toby. "It's. . . it's. . ."

"Weird?" said Jayne.

"That's the word I was looking for," said Toby. "Weird. Definitely weird."

"And how did he get the teddy bear into Cedric's house?" said Charlotte. "And why put it *there*, of all places?"

As they arrived back at Mr Elliott's house and started making their way through the Sea of Debris, Cedric's head popped over the next-door fence.

"We've got a secret," he said. "And you'll never guess what it is."

"It's lucky we're not interested in your stupid secrets, then, isn't it?" said Ben.

Boff switched to Naitabal language.

"*Ister-ming Elliott's-eng an-vung is-ing ack-bang.*"

"We've got a secret language as well," said Cedric, not to be left out.

"Really?" said Charlotte. "It must be the way you speak English, I suppose, because we can never understand what you're talking about."

The Naitabals had turned by this time and were following Boff in a line towards Mr Elliott's back door. Boff knocked politely, the door opened, and they all trooped inside.

"Hello, Mr Elliott. Not working this afternoon?"

"Finished that job, mates. Can't start the next one till next week. What can I do fer you today?"

"You know you told us about the corner of Cedric's house that you built diagonally to miss the dog's grave?" said Boff. The others listened, wondering what Boff was going to ask.

"Yuss, mate."

"Were they the same people who sold the house to Mr and Mrs Morgan?"

"Coo, no, not them. I remember it like yesterday as it was only next door, like. No, those people sold it to a man called Mr Leonard, and Mr Leonard did a bit of work in it and then sold it six months later to the Morgans. Does that help?"

Mr Elliott knew it must have helped. Just before he'd answered the question he'd been looking at a row of interested faces. Now he found himself looking at a row of gaping holes, like birds' nests in a sand bank.

"Yuss, I can see it does help," he said, answering his own question. "You don't have to tell me any of yer secrets, mates," he added, "but if there's anything more you want to know, just ask."

"What did Mr Leonard look like?" said Boff.

"Elderly," said Mr Elliott. "Some people'd say old. About seventy, I'd say. White hair. White beard. Shortish, like me. Tidy. Wore a suit and a shirt and tie."

"Thank you," said Boff.

"Thanks, Mr Elliott," said the others. They all bade him

farewell and made their way back to the Naitabal tree-house in silence.

"Well, it's not *our* Mr Leonard," said Charlotte. "He looks nothing like that, and he certainly couldn't have been seventy all those years ago when Cedric moved in, because he's only coming up to retiring at sixty-five now!"

Boff was shaking his head.

"The sooner we can get into Deep Shadow Cottage," he said, "the better!"

But someone else was inside Deep Shadow Cottage, even as Boff said the words.

Mrs Josie Fern had succeeded in persuading the estate agent to lend her the keys so she could get 'a long, atmospheric feel for the place on her own'. But rather than feeling any atmosphere, Mrs Fern was feeling drawers and cupboards and furniture and letter racks and paperwork and boxes. Feeling anything, in fact, that might have belonged to her ex-husband. Since the shocking events that had led to his disappearance, it had taken her the whole six or seven years to track him down. Now she'd found him, but only because he was dead. Dead for eight days, after living in the cottage in secret for the missing years. Even now she wondered if she was too late to find what she was looking for.

She found nothing that interested her, and nothing gave her any clues, with one exception. She was intrigued by the locked cellar door. She tried her best to pick the lock, without success, and even gave it a few strong kicks, but it was a door that opened outwards and the door was tight against the frame.

After that, she spent some time looking round the little overgrown garden enclosed by the stone wall that encircled the cottage, but found nothing suspicious.

She left soon after, determined to make the little estate

102

agent sort out a key to the cellar.

Mr Leonard rang Boff that evening. He had spoken to the estate agent and told him that the Naitabals would be cleaning and tidying the cottage and perhaps doing some decorating as well. Boff could collect a front door key from the agent the following day.

The only problem was that the Naitabals had all asked their parents if they could help Mr Leonard by cleaning and decorating his cottage in the woods, and each set of parents, except Toby's, hadn't liked the idea.

"We don't mind you playing in the woods and running through them together," Jayne's mother had said, "but being inside an isolated cottage is different. It's not so easy to scream and run away if there's trouble. No one would hear you inside the cottage."

"But we'd *all* be there!" Jayne had protested, but to no avail.

The other Naitabals' parents had similar views.

"You're safe in your tree-house, even at night," they said, "because you're locked in and you're safe in the gardens. But a strange cottage in the middle of the woods with strange people coming to view it. . . Sorry, not this one."

"We could lock ourselves in. . . and borrow a mobile phone. . .?

"We'd love you to help this Mr Leonard with his claustrophobia, but – well, we don't know him, either, do we? Not like Mr Elliott. . ."

Early the following morning, Mr Elliott opened his front door to find all five Naitabals standing in a line. It was Jayne who spoke, wearing her sweetest smile.

"Mr Elliott. . ."

"Yuss, that's me, mates." At that moment he saw the hedge next door moving as if it contained some large animal.

"Come in, come in," he added, pointing. "Hedges have ears."

They shuffled into the hallway, and as soon as Toby had closed the front door behind them, Jayne shone her sweet smile on Mr Elliott again.

"Mr Elliott. . ."

"Yuss, mate. It's still me."

"You know you said you didn't have another job to start for a few days. . ."

"Yurse. That's right. Man o' leisure, that's me. It'll take me two days to pay all me bills."

"Well. . ."

"Come on. Gurgitate it. It's in there somewhere."

"We wondered if you would teach us how to decorate a cottage. . ."

"Coo! I got the whole story now! Let me see if I'm right. You want to investigate that secret in Deep Shadow Cottage, and you offered to decorate it so's you could all do some legal snooping, like, and now your parents have said they ain't lettin' you loose in the middle of the woods in a strange cottage all on your own? Am I right?"

Jayne looked shamefaced.

"Yes, Mr Elliott."

"Coo! I can read you lot like a road sign. Dangerous corner!"

"Does that mean you will, Mr Elliott?" said Jayne, cheering up again.

"'Course I will. I'd much rather be watching you lot tryin' to hang wallpaper than sitting at home here payin' bills!"

"Mr Elliott, you're wonderful!" said Charlotte and Jayne together.

"I know," said Mr Elliott. "But don't keep tellin' me, or me head'll swell up and I'll be top-heavy for me ladders."

Half an hour later, the Naitabals and Mr Elliott arrived at Deep Shadow Cottage with big bags of decorating tools.

While Mr Elliott inspected the outside of the property, the Naitabals went inside and down into the basement to see for themselves the photocopying equipment that Jayne and Charlotte had uncovered. There was nothing else in the cellar that seemed significant, and they didn't spend too much time down there in case the estate agent brought anyone to view the house and caught them.

Next it was the attic.

The hatch that led into the attic was at the top of the stairs. There was a long hook hanging behind the door of the adjacent room, and when the trap-door was pushed once, the catch was freed and the door could be carefully lowered with the hook.

Even though the Naitabals had permission – Mr Leonard's blessing, in fact – to be in the house, and to look for the missing half-sheet of paper, they didn't want to be caught snooping in the attic. They didn't want anyone else to get the idea there might be something interesting up there. So they took it in turns to go on sentry duty.

Mr Elliott quickly decided that the outside of the cottage needed cleaning and re-painting, including all the windows and doors. It was his perfect solution for looking after the Naitabals, but at the same time keeping out of their way. Like the true friend he was, he promised to bang on the windows as soon as he saw anyone approaching.

Being on sentry duty meant beginning the cleaning process, but being ready to rush upstairs and tell the others the moment Mr Elliott knocked on a window. Charlotte started cleaning near the front door and Toby at the back, while Boff fetched a stepladder from a cupboard in the kitchen. Then he, Jayne and Ben climbed through the hatch and into the dark space at the top of the house. There was no electric light in the roof void, so they each carried a Naitabal torch.

"Well, we all know the riddle off by heart," said Boff. "*Go*

*to the top of my nest, as low as you can be. In limb, o hollow
chest, one, two, three."*

"I don't understand the first line, to start with," said Jayne.
"How can we go to the top and be as low as we can be?"

"'In limb, o hollow chest' sounds suspiciously like an
anagram to me," said Ben.

"We don't even know what sort of thing we're looking
for," said Jayne.

They stood carefully on the joists surrounding the hatch
opening and all three of them flashed their torches round like
a battery of wartime searchlights. At first glance the attic
seemed empty.

"Well, most other attics I've been in. . ." began Ben.

"Meaning just your one, at home?" put in Jayne.

". . .Well, yes, okay. *Our* attic's packed with stuff. We
can hardly get in it. This is the only one I've *heard* of being
empty."

"Ours is full of junk as well," Jayne admitted. "If anyone
hasn't got room for something it goes in a box and straight
into the attic. There's more stuff in our attic than the rest of
the house."

By this time Boff had started moving to one end, taking
care to step on top of the joists and not put his foot through
one of the ceilings.

"That *would* be a dead give-away," he said, warning the
others before they set out in different directions.

"There isn't even a water tank," said Ben.

"The water's pumped up in the kitchen by hand," said
Boff. "Charlotte said. It comes from an underground
storage tank that catches rain water."

"There isn't any insulation stuff, either," said Ben. "It's
ten centimetres thick in our loft."

"This must be a cold house in the winter," said Jayne,
shivering.

The three of them explored the whole space, right into each

corner, but there was absolutely nothing to find.   No
packages, no boxes, no plastic bags tied up with waterproof
string – nothing.

"There's no roofing felt under the tiles, either," said Boff,
"so there's no scope for hiding anything there, either."

"I can't see where anyone could hide anything up here,"
said Ben, making his way back to the trap-door. "Come on,
Jayne, let's go on sentry duty and let Charlotte and Toby
have a look."

They swapped over, but the story from the new explorers
was just the same. Ten minutes later they were all down, the
trap-door closed, the stepladder returned to its cupboard, to
give them time to think. They all rolled up their sleeves and
continued spring-cleaning.   They could hear Mr Elliott
whistling a tune, along with the sounds of him rubbing down
the paintwork outside.

"At least nobody else is going to find it," said Ben,
"whatever it is."

The others agreed that it was a comforting thought.

After more discussion it was decided that they should hide
the photocopying plates of £50 notes that were in the cellar,
before the estate agent arranged to bring in a locksmith or
break down the door. But the question was, where to hide
them?

"We could take them home," said Ben, grinning.

"Oh, yes," said Charlotte, guessing what he was thinking.
"And unstick the twelve £50 notes and spend them!"

"They don't belong to us, of course," said Boff. "They're
part of the house. They belong to Mr Leonard."

Another trip to the basement revealed a good hiding place
behind a filing cabinet that was awkward to get at under the
steps.

"No one will find them there unless they're really
looking," said Charlotte. "And why should anyone be really
looking?"

*

"We've got to examine every inch of the attic," Boff said at last, when they were sitting round the kitchen table having refreshments. They had made two rooms as clean as glass beads, and they were all ready to solve the mystery of the teddy bear's riddle. Mr Elliott sat quietly with his big mug of tea and didn't interfere or ask questions.

"The first thing we've got to do," said Boff, "is to look for writing on the joists on the *floor* of the attic. The first line that says *'go to the top of my nest'* – that *must* mean the attic. *'As low as you can be'* – that *must* mean the floor of the attic. And the only things on the floor in this attic are the wooden joists that we have to walk on, and the ceiling laths and plaster in between. So I think we should start at one end and use our torches to see if anything's written anywhere at all."

"I see what you mean," said Ben. "There's nothing *hidden*, because there's nothing in the attic to hide behind, except dust. So it must be something written – another clue, perhaps."

Once again, with Mr Elliott outside, two of the Naitabals carried on cleaning downstairs while the other three crawled on the joists on their knees looking for the message that they hoped was written somewhere. After an hour and a half and several changes of teams, they had covered the entire attic floor and found nothing. Everyone's hair was full of cobwebs, and their clothes were smeared with black, gritty dust.

They stopped, closed the attic door, cleaned themselves as best they could, called Mr Elliott, and surrounded more cups of tea in the kitchen.

"So what's next?" said Charlotte. "It's beginning to look like a wild chest chase."

"The next place where you're as low as you can be is under the eaves," said Boff, "where the floor of the attic meets the roof at the sides. Perhaps the message is there, on the back of a slate, or on one of the roof joists, or on the battens that the slates are nailed on to."

"It's clever of you to know the names of everything," said Jayne. "I thought they were all just bits of wood."

"I helped my dad fix some slates once," said Boff, "when we had scaffolding up to do new guttering and fascia boards. He taught me all the names."

An hour later, they were back in the kitchen again, but this time Mr Elliott had volunteered to have his tea outside while he carried on working. The Naitabals had found nothing. They'd checked every inch of the back of every visible slate, every roof joist and every batten, but apart from scribbled measurements from carpenters, there was nothing to be seen at all.

"Well, if there's anything in *that* attic," said Toby, wiping some dusty cobwebs out of his mouth, "it's the best hiding place I've ever heard of."

"As low as you can be. . ." murmured Charlotte. "What else can it mean?"

"I hope 'go to the top of my nest' doesn't mean the roof," said Jayne. "I'm definitely not going up there."

Boff shook his head.

"I'm sure it can't mean the roof."

"What about the next line?" said Jayne. "We haven't thought about that much. 'In limb, o hollow chest. . .' "

"I still think it's an anagram," said Ben. "Mix up the letters and we'll have the message."

Boff was thinking.

"The trouble is," he said, "I keep thinking the limb is something to do with a leg. Perhaps it isn't."

"I don't see that it helps much whether it's a leg or an arm," said Toby.

Boff buried himself in thought again, then said suddenly, "Has anyone got a dictionary?"

"Oh, yes, Boff," said Ben. "We carry dictionaries round with us all the time."

"There are some reference books in the sitting-room," said Jayne. "I noticed them when I was dusting. I'll go and see if there's a dictionary."

She came back beaming, clutching a big fat book.

"It's old, but it'll probably do."

Boff took it, flipped open the pages, and read.

"*Limb. One: Arm or leg. Two: A branch of a tree. Three: An edge or border, as in the graduated edge of a sextant.*"

"Yes," said Ben. "I remember now. When you're out on a limb, you're on your own – out on the end of a tree branch, I suppose."

But Boff was reading further on, his eyes scanning the words that followed.

"*Limbo,*" he said suddenly. "*A place of waiting in the world beyond for the souls of those not properly qualified for heaven.*"

"Sounds like us," said Charlotte.

"*Ariosta: a place of all last things; Milton: the paradise of fools; Shakespeare: hell itself.*"

"What's all that supposed to mean?" said Toby, screwing up his face. "Doesn't it say anything about the dance?"

Boff looked up sharply. He suddenly felt a tingling wave travel up his back and through his hair.

"Toby! You've got it!"

Toby looked bewildered.

"I have?"

"Well, you might have," admitted Boff. "This dictionary is so old, it hasn't got limbo dancing in it."

"What's a limbo dance?" said Jayne.

"It's a dance they do in Africa or the West Indies or somewhere. . ." said Toby.

"The West Indies," said Boff.

". . .where they have to lean backwards and dance forwards

110

under a pole, which gets put down lower and lower."

"It's the opposite of a high jump," said Ben. "A low slump."

The others laughed. They laughed again as Toby demonstrated by limbo dancing under the kitchen table. Then he lost his balance halfway through, grabbed the table legs, and nearly turned the whole thing over.

"Anyway," he said, getting up and dusting himself off, "it's difficult."

"That's because," said Boff slowly, *"you were as low as you could be!"* He was staring at Toby, and the other Naitabals knew he was excited, even though he wasn't jumping up and down. "I bet you anything you like. . ." he started to say, then trailed off.

"Boff!" said Charlotte. "Don't do this to us! Tell us!"

Boff turned his head quickly, scraped his chair backwards on the kitchen floor and stood up.

"Lock the front and back doors," he said, "and bolt them." It was a command, but nobody minded, it was just Boff's way of showing his excitement. "But ask Mr Elliott if he minds. If a vehicle comes, we'll hear it up in the loft, but we might not hear Mr Elliott banging on the window to warn us."

The others rushed to make the cottage secure. Mr Elliott guessed they were all going into the attic and didn't mind them bolting the doors and windows so no one could surprise them and get in.

Then the Naitabals all followed Boff into the attic for the umpteenth time.

CHAPTER ELEVEN

Iscovery-dang

The morning had started cold, and Cedric and Doris had been confined to their house, at least until Mrs Morgan was satisfied that it was warm enough for them to go out. She didn't want them to have, as she called it, a 'prelapse'. As soon as the day promised warmth and sunshine she finally gave them their freedom.

Being confined to barracks for so long meant they had no idea where the Naitabals had gone, so the first place they visited was their own tree-house, with Andy and Amanda, to await the Naitabals' return.

Doris had been doing a lot of thinking during their imprisonment, as she put it. Her sense of suspicion and irritation had been growing steadily ever since Margery had departed with the teddy bear. She attacked Cedric as soon as they were back in their favourite tree.

"How did that Margery know there was a teddy bear hidden in a box under your floorboards?" she demanded.

"Charlotte made it go there using her special powers," said Cedric.

"Don't talk rot," snapped Doris. "Magic powers!" She was almost spitting. "There's more to it than magic powers! Magic con-trick more likely!"

"How did she do it, then, if you're so clever?"

"How should I know? That's what I just asked you, you idiot! I wouldn't have asked you how she did it if I knew how she did it myself, would I?"

Andy and Amanda seemed disappointed. They had both been impressed by the magic.

"She used the earth's magnetic compass," said Amanda. "That's why she can only move things from south to north."

"Yeah," said Andy. Compasses are magic, aren't they?"

Doris glared at them.

"No one in the world has ever moved anything to anywhere just using the power of their mind," she shouted. "I only believed it when Charlotte did it because I couldn't believe there'd be anything there."

"That makes sense," said Cedric sarcastically. "You only believed it because you didn't believe it."

"You know what I mean. I was so impressed I didn't have time to think."

Andy had been thinking.

"Those magicians on stage move people using the power of their mind," he said. "They move people from one cabinet to another."

Doris glared at Andy, almost bereft of speech.

"They. . .!" she began, then gave up and started again. "It's a *trick*, Andy. Just like Charlotte's was a trick, but I don't know how she did it."

"She moved the drawers from the chest as well," Amanda reminded her. "She hadn't even been in the room that time."

Doris had no answer for that one. She furrowed her brows together and glared at the three of them.

"I still think that was *Cedric*," she said, staring at him, daring him to deny it.

"It was *you*," he retorted. "You did it when you came into my room half asleep. Sleep-moving drawers, that's what you were doing."

"I wasn't."

"You were."

"I wasn't."

"You were. I *saw* you doing it."

"Liar."

"Anyway," said Cedric, suddenly bored with the argument,

113

"what are we going to do about it?"

"We want that teddy back, to start with," said Doris.

"It's not ours."

"Yes it is. There's no way they could have put that teddy under the floorboards, but *they knew it was there*. That means it was there all the time, and *that* means it was in the house when we bought it, and *that* means it belongs to *us*!"

"So what are we going to do, then?"

"You're supposed to be the leader of this gang, Cedric, but I'll tell you what you're all going to do!"

"What?"

"Follow me, that's what."

Doris was halfway out of the tree by this time, and the other three scrambled to catch up with her.

"Doris. . ."

But Doris's reddening ears were closed. She marched them up the garden, through the side gate, out on to the pavement, and up the path to Charlotte's front door. She stabbed a plump, curved thumb on the bell.

"Doris. . ." hissed Cedric.

"Shut up!" Doris hissed back.

Then the door opened and Mrs Maddison stood there in surprise, a grown-up version of Charlotte.

"Hello, Doris; Amanda; Cedric; Andy. To what do I owe this pleasure?"

"Hello Mrs Maddison," said Doris. At the same moment Harry rushed up behind his mother and crashed into her legs, making her sway with the impact. "Could we speak to Margery, please?"

Cedric realised with horror what his sister was up to, and pulled anxiously on her elbow.

"We promised. . ." he hissed in her ear.

Mrs Maddison leaned forward to listen more carefully.

"Did you say *Margery*?"

"Yes. Margery. Charlotte's identical twin sister."

Cedric tried to pull Doris backwards as a burst of laughter escaped Mrs Maddison.

"Charlotte's what?" she giggled.

"Identical twin sister," repeated Doris firmly. "We know it's a secret," she added, pushing Cedric off the step, "and we promise not to tell anyone else, but we really want to talk to her about our teddy bear."

A flicker of light dawned in Mrs Maddison's eyes.

"Do you mean the Margery who wears a red dress and has her hair down?"

"Yes."

"Ah. In that case, she's not here at the moment," said Mrs Maddison truthfully. "Can I give her a message?"

"No, thanks," said Doris. "We'll ask Charlotte instead. Do you know where she is?"

"She's just gone back with the others. They're spring-cleaning the cottage in the woods that's for sale."

"Thanks, Mrs Maddison," said Doris. "Goodbye. Goodbye, Harry."

"NOT HARRY!" Harry screamed. "BILLY!"

Mrs Maddison laughed and closed the door. The Igmopong shouted "Yes!" and ran across the road into the woods.

The Naitabals stood two on each side of Boff as he shone his torch on the horizontal cross-beams in the attic. The cross-beams supported the sloping roof beams from side to side, holding them together, like the middle line in the capital letter 'A'.

"You can see how low they are," Boff said. "Most people would climb *over* them. We did, didn't we, when we were moving from one end to the other – we climbed *over* them."

"So what?" said Ben.

"Show me how you go under it, Ben."

Ben obliged. He walked carefully on the joists towards the

first cross-beam, then stooped forwards. He steadied himself
with one hand on the cross-beam itself and the other on the
joist at his feet, then swung underneath, his back just
brushing the underside of the beam.

"See?" said Boff. "Even if someone goes *under* one, they
wouldn't notice."

"Boff!" said Charlotte. "Notice *what*?"

"How low they are, of course. How low you'd have to be
to limbo under one of them. As low as you can be!"

"I'm sorry," said Jayne. "I can't see how it makes any
difference whether you limbo under a beam or crawl under
it, or pretend to be a fairy and fly under it. What are you
trying to tell us, Boff?"

"Stay here!" said Boff. He stepped towards the first A-
section, then bent down from his waist until he was looking
at the beam's underside, then shone his torch upwards on it.
He seemed disappointed, and moved forward to the next one,
calling back to them.

"Unless you *limbo*," he said, "*you don't see the underside
of the beam!*"

He stopped at the next one, bent low, and twisted his head
and torch to survey the underside. They saw his torch beam
travel slowly along its length, then suddenly stop as Boff
gave a yell.

"*That's it!*" he shouted. "*It's here!*"

The others stayed balanced round the attic trap-door,
waiting for Boff to tell them exactly what was where. But
instead of telling them, he was turning himself over, trying to
lie on his back across the uncomfortable joists to look up at
the cross-beam. He was finding it painful, and twisted back
on to his knees again. Now he was bending low, craning his
neck and twisting from side to side, shining his torch the
length of the beam, tapping it with his knuckles, and
whispering, "Wow!"

Charlotte's patience was the first to run out.

"Boff. Excuse us, but we're here as well, you know. Will you kindly tell us what you've found and what's so 'Wow' about it?"

Boff switched off his torch and looked at them upside down from between his legs, his glasses hanging down over his forehead.

"It's so clever," he said. "No one could ever find it in a million years unless they had the clue, like we did."

"Yes, Boff, but. . ." Charlotte's voice began sounding like a thundery afternoon on Tabletop Mountain, so Boff forestalled her and explained.

"Underneath this beam," he said, manoeuvring himself upright, turning to face them, and tapping the timber with his torch, "there's a line of those pirate figures. They're burned into the wood. How many were there on the chest that had the teddy in?"

"Three at each end," said Toby straight away, four along each side, and one in the middle."

"That's fifteen," said Jayne.

"That's how many are under this beam," said Boff. "Fifteen of them."

"*Fifteen men on the dead man's chest!*" hissed Ben. "The chest we found with the teddy bear in!"

"Exactly," said Boff. "Come and look at the beam. See how it's been done."

"How *what's* been done, Boff?"

"Come and see."

They gravitated towards Boff in the dim light. One by one they swung their heads down and looked up at the underside of the wood.

"Can you see the fifteen pirates?" Boff said, as each of them took their turn. "Now look closer all along the underside. Can you see two thin lines, about a centimetre from the edges, running along its length?"

It was only when they had all bent double and twisted

themselves upwards and seen the pirates and the lines, that Boff told them what it must mean.

"I reckon it means," he said, "*that this beam is hollow*!"

"What??"

"*In limb, o hollow chest.* Don't you see the double meaning? In Limbo – meaning *go under it so that you're looking up at the beam*, and In limb, meaning something's inside the branch – inside the wood. And then the words 'hollow chest' to confirm it. *Fifteen men on the dead man's chest*! Wow! It's so brilliant a hiding place, I can't believe it!"

Boff was still really excited, while the others were both excited and impressed.

"So now," said Ben, "we've got to find out what's inside it."

"That's right," said Toby cheerfully. "Let's saw through it and make the house fall down."

"I've tried tapping it, but it doesn't sound hollow," said Boff, tapping it again along its length and listening.

"I think," said Charlotte, sounding horribly sensible, "that we ought to go downstairs, close the attic for a while, and think about the next move before we rush into anything. If one of the beams *is* hollow, Toby's right – are we going to saw the attic down to see what's inside it? Come on. Let's go and clean another room and talk about it down there."

Everyone knew that Charlotte was right. The excitement of Boff's discovery had also made them forget where they were and what they were supposed to be doing for Mr Leonard.

"You're right," said Boff. "Come on."

By the time the third room had been spring-cleaned, the Naitabals had worked out the safest way to see if the beam in the attic was really hollow. Boff's theory was that the beam had been hollowed out like an upside down trough, with the

118

middle sawn out, cut down, and the top part glued back like a lid. That explained the two lines near the edges. The beam had then been replaced in the attic upside down so no one could see the mark of the pirates or the glue-joins in the 'lid' – unless they limboed underneath – which was impossible in an attic on joists that ran the wrong way!

The next problem had been how to test the theory.

"We can't saw the beam in half," said Ben. "The roof might fall down."

"I've got a feeling the beam was added later," said Boff. "Anyway, if it's hollow, it's not going to be adding much strength to the roof, is it?"

"We'll have to drill a hole in it, then," said Jayne. "That'll tell us if it's hollow."

"And what if it is?" said Charlotte. "What then?"

"If those long lines underneath are where the beam was hollowed out, and the lid put back," said Jayne innocently, "can't we just get a chisel and prise off the lid?"

"Jayne's right," said Ben.

"No one would be able to see we'd touched anything if it just comes out," Jayne added. "Or even if it doesn't."

Everyone liked Jayne's idea, but there was nothing they could do for a while. It was already lunch-time, and their parents would be expecting them home.

When they returned after lunch, Charlotte and Boff were armed with carrier bags containing even more of Mr Elliott's tools – two chisels, two hammers, two big screwdrivers, a brace and bit, and some long screws and nails.

They locked all the doors and windows, and while Mr Elliott helped Toby and Jayne move furniture ready for decorating, Boff, Ben and Charlotte went into the attic. They took the tools and three torches with them, and began the exciting task of investigating the beam.

In the end it didn't take very long. To make it easier, they found two planks, took them up into the attic with them, and laid them across the joists underneath the beam to make a comfortable place to lie down. Then, lying on her back on the planks, with Ben and Boff shining torches for her, Charlotte (who'd won the toss) inserted a chisel in the line near the edge of the beam underneath. She angled it slightly to give it some leverage, then gave it a few taps with the hammer.

She discovered straight away that the upside down 'lid' underneath the beam had not been glued in, but wedged. As she tapped the chisel and moved it along the line, so the beam started opening underneath.

Ben and Boff were both watching, but Charlotte was still shouting progress in a suppressed whisper.

"It's coming loose, look!" Tap, tap, tap. "The whole strip's moving – all along the beam!"

Moments later, Charlotte was able to grasp the loosened end of the 'lid' with one hand and pull it down towards her. With the other hand she reached inside, while Ben tried to shine his torch in at the same time.

"Is there anything there?" he said. "Can you see?"

At last Charlotte squeaked as her fingers gripped something inside the beam. When she eased it out, and Ben and Boff's torches flooded it with light, they simply couldn't believe their eyes.

"*Oh. . . my. . . quadruplicate. . . wow!*" breathed Charlotte.

CHAPTER TWELVE

Emptation-tong

The Igmopong ducked down and began to creep towards Deep Shadow Cottage as soon as they were in sight of its roof. They managed to keep below the level of the wall, out of sight. It was only when they reached the gate that led to its front door that they paused.

"Can you see anything?" said Cedric to Doris, who was at the front.

"Yes. A house," said Doris sarcastically.

"No, I mean, can you see any of the Naitabals?"

"No. But I can hear banging."

"So can I," said Andy.

"And me," said Amanda.

"Why are we hiding?" said Cedric suddenly. "I thought you said we were coming to get our teddy bear back?"

"We won't get it back if we ask for it," said Doris. "We've come to *take it* back."

The Igmopong watched and waited.

Mrs Josie Fern walked up the track leading to Deep Shadow Cottage. Nearby, her poodle zig-zagged from side to side, ran ahead, hung back, sniffed and did everything expected of a dog on its walk. Mrs Fern was still feeling disappointed that she had found nothing in her ex-husband's rented cottage that gave her any clue as to how he had lived since he had disappeared all those years ago, leaving her penniless. Deep in her heart, although she had witnessed his last terrible deed, she wanted to know if he had *died* penniless, too, or whether there was something she could

121

still lay her hands on.

The only room she had failed to look in was the cellar. As she clutched the front door key in her pocket, she had already decided to enter the cellar at all costs, cellar key or no cellar key. Mrs Josie Fern was suspicious of doors that were locked. Anyway, one really good wrench with a crowbar would break the lock, and locks could easily be replaced.

As she neared the cottage, she was surprised to the see a group of children huddled by the wall near the front door. They all had their backs to her.

She spoke suddenly and made them all jump.

"Are you looking for something?" she said.

The Igmopong, taken completely by surprise, almost left the ground in fright. They turned to discover a good-looking woman standing in the rutted track, holding a strange combination of poodle and steel crowbar.

"They took our teddy bear," garbled Doris, who was the first to recover the power of speech. "And we want it back. She told us it belonged to her twin sister," Doris blurted on, "but we think it's been under the floorboards for years, and anyway it had 'Sarah's Little Treasure' written on the box and a note inside saying 'love from Deedy' so we don't think it was anything to do with her sister at all, because her name's Margery."

Both the poodle and Mrs Josie Fern had pricked up their ears. What had made the poodle prick up its ears was the sight of a squirrel moving in the branches of a nearby tree. What had made Mrs Josie Fern prick up her ears was not the name Sarah – there were thousands of children called Sarah who owned teddy bears. The fact that her ex-husband had a favourite niece called Sarah was neither here nor there, and not in the least ear-pricking material. What had made Mrs Josie Fern prick up her ears was the mention of 'Deedy'. Her ex-husband was known to his favourite niece as 'Uncle

Deedy', because of his initials, D.D. Fern. There was no chance that this Sarah and this 'Deedy' could be anyone else.

Suddenly Mrs Josie Fern was very interested in this teddy bear, and especially in the fact that it had been hidden for several years.

"Who did you say took your teddy bear?"

"The stupid old Naitabals."

"And who exactly are the. . . Naitabals?"

"Just a stupid gang of kids," said Doris.

"Are they inside the cottage now?"

"Yes. They've been hammering for ages."

"What exactly are they doing in the house? Are they supposed to be in there?"

"Charlotte's mum said they're cleaning it. It was Charlotte's sister who took the teddy bear."

"I see. Well, I must meet these house-cleaning Naitabals."

The woman pushed past them and inserted the estate agent's key into the front door lock. As she turned it, she discovered that the door was bolted from the inside. At the same moment the surprised face of a girl appeared, looking out at them all through the glass.

At first, Boff, Ben and Charlotte simply couldn't believe what they were looking at. The bundle that Charlotte was holding in her hand was nothing less than a bundle of banknotes – a bundle of £50 banknotes, crisp and new and weighty and clean.

"Are they *real*?" whispered Ben hoarsely, his voice cracked with excitement and disbelief.

Charlotte, her hands quivering in the torchlight, flicked through the bundle. The notes were secured with a thick brown paper band.

"They look real to me," said Charlotte, still lying flat on her back.

They all wanted to hold them and feel them. They took it

in turns to flick through the bundle. Ben pulled out one of the crisp notes and held it up against the light of two torches.

"I can see the watermark and the metal band," he said. "It looks real enough to me. We'll have to see them in daylight to make sure."

"How many are there?" said Boff.

"About a hundred, at a guess," said Charlotte. "That's. . ." she calculated, "that's. . . *five thousand pounds!!*"

Their faces shone with pleasure in the torchlight.

"I'll count them," said Ben, eagerly. He licked his fingers and started counting through the bundle. "One, two, three. . ."

"*One, two, three* – !" said Boff suddenly, reminding himself of the rhyming clue. "In limb, o hollow chest, *one, two, three.* . . There must be *two more* in there, Charlotte!"

Charlotte levered the long plug of the beam downwards from the end and slid her forearm inside.

"Yes! There's another one! Boff! That's *ten* thousand pounds! *I can't believe it!*"

But none of them had time to believe anything for much longer. At that moment a whispered shout from below came up through the attic door, interrupting Ben's note-count at thirty-seven. It was Jayne's voice, and it sounded really urgent.

"Someone's here! Quick! They've got a key! We'll have to unbolt the door for them!"

Without a second's hesitation Charlotte released the second hidden bundle, grabbed the first one from Ben and stuffed it back into the hollow beam. Ben stuffed the single note they'd pulled from the bundle into his pocket, while Boff knelt with the hammer, ready to wedge the 'lid' of the beam back into place. As Charlotte rolled out of the way, Boff gave three good upward bangs, and the beam was suddenly transformed to its previous innocent-looking self.

"Shall I open?" hissed Jayne.

"Thirty seconds," said Boff.

Now they could hear a woman's raised voice demanding that the door be opened. Without a word, they moved the planks away from the tell-tale beam and laid them down quietly over the bag of tools that Boff had placed in the space between two joists. Thirty seconds after that, they were all down on the landing, the ladder was stowed away, and Jayne was shooting open the bolt on the front door.

Mr Elliott, sensing trouble, had wandered into the hallway.

"Why didn't you open the door straight away?" said a woman's voice, complaining.

Before Jayne could answer, the woman continued.

"Is there someone called Charlotte here?"

"Yes," said Toby, who was with Jayne at the front door.

"May I speak with her, please?"

Boff, Ben and Charlotte hurried down the stairs, brushing themselves off as they went. They were surprised to find not only the woman in the hall, but the Igmopong pressed in behind her as well. The hall was only just big enough for eleven people.

"Hello," said Charlotte through the crush. "I'm Charlotte. Can I help?"

"I understand from this child" – the woman extracted an arm and indicated Doris – "that you have obtained a teddy bear from her house under false pretences. Well, *my name is Sarah*, the teddy bear belongs to me, and I would like it back – now, please."

Charlotte was so shocked, she lost the power of speech altogether for a few seconds.

"Did you hear me?" said the woman.

"I – I'm afraid I haven't got it," lied Charlotte.

"Oh? Then where is it?"

"My twin sister Margery's got it," said Charlotte, inspired at last. "And she's gone away."

The other Naitabals turned to Charlotte in shocked

125

admiration. Mr Elliott examined some cracks he'd noticed in the wall plaster.

"Where does she live?"

"In Scotland," said Charlotte promptly. "Would you like me to telephone her and ask her to send it back?"

"Yes, I would. And I hope you're not playing games with me, young lady. Here's where I'm staying." She fumbled in her handbag, wrote something on a card, and handed it over. "If I don't get this teddy bear back in two days, I'll call the police, do you understand?"

"Yes," said Charlotte.

The woman turned on her heel, rummaged her way through the Igmopong, and disappeared up the track. The Igmopong rushed after her, falling over each other in their haste to escape from the scene as quickly as possible.

Mr Elliott slipped unobtrusively into the living-room. The Naitabals were in disarray, staring after the departing delegation, except for Boff, who stood looking confidently round at his friends.

"That's funny," he said.

"What's funny?" said Jayne. "Nothing's funny at the moment."

"Yes it is," said Boff. "First, there's what Charlotte and Ben and I have found in the attic. That's *really* funny. And then there's that woman."

"What about her?"

"Well, when I was in the estate agent's yesterday, she came in just as I was leaving. She didn't say her name was Sarah then. She told *them* her name was Josie Fern."

"Well!" said Charlotte. "What a cheek, then!"

"It's pretty obvious who told her about the teddy bear," said Ben. "You can't trust the Igmopong for a second."

"I wonder who she really is?" said Jayne. "This Josie Fern. If she's so interested in the teddy bear, she must know something about this Sarah."

126

For a few moments, the Naitabals didn't know what to do next. Ben, Charlotte and Boff were full of suppressed excitement over what they had found in the attic. Jayne was feeling guilty over not seeing the visitors sooner, and Charlotte was feeling annoyed at being spoken to so rudely by the woman. Now she was even crosser because the woman wasn't Sarah at all.

Toby, who had been on guard at the back door, was the only one who knew what he wanted to do next. He wanted to know what the others had found in the attic, but didn't sense it was the right moment to ask.

Charlotte's cheeks had coloured up, and she was already planning revenge.

"If she wants a teddy bear," she exclaimed furiously, "she can *have* a teddy bear! And as for the *Igmopong*. . ." She gritted her teeth and left the sentence unfinished.

"Listen!" said Toby cheerfully, choosing his moment. "Never mind that now. Why don't you show Jayne and me what you found in the attic? We're dying to know."

"Yes!" said Charlotte, brightening. "Sorry, both. You won't believe *this* in a *million years!*"

As none of them wanted a repeat of the panic, it was decided that they would go into the attic in twos. First Boff and Charlotte went up to rearrange the planks and make ready the hammer and chisel. To avoid complications, they brought down any tools they didn't need. Then Charlotte took Jayne up, then Ben took Toby up. Every one of them found it difficult to believe what they had found.

Mr Elliott was working outside again when Ben and Toby came down carrying the plastic bag they had filled with the bundles of banknotes. They drew the curtains in the kitchen before tipping on to the table the entire contents of the hollow beam. As they thudded on to the table, with some bouncing on to the floor, the Naitabals were literally stunned. There were *twenty* packets of banknotes, not just three, and each packet contained one hundred £50 notes. It didn't take a maths genius to work out that each packet contained £5000. With twenty bundles, the Naitabals found themselves in the darkened kitchen staring at no less than £100,000 in cash.

Instinctively, they turned to Boff, but for once Boff was too stunned to think.

"Boff. . . what are we going to do. . .?"

"I – I don't know. . ."

"Do you think we should tell Mr Elliott?" said Ben. "He's been really good keeping out of the way and everything, but. . ."

"Not yet," said Charlotte. "Let's think first."

They were all too weak-kneed to stand up any longer, so they all dragged chairs towards the plain wooden table and sat down, staring at the pile of money. It was more than any of them had ever seen in their lives before, and probably more than they would ever see again.

But that wasn't the end.

Toby eventually picked up a bundle and started counting the notes, just as Ben had done earlier, "One, two, three. . ." Boff, reminded, looked up suddenly and turned his head towards each of the others in turn.

"One, two, three. . ." he said again. "There should only have been *three* bundles. But there are *twenty*."

"So what, Boff?" Toby said, and stopped counting. He hadn't been in the attic when Boff had said the words before.

"*In limb, o hollow chest, one, two, three*," Boff repeated the rhyme from the teddy bear. "What does 'one, two, three' mean if it doesn't mean three bundles of banknotes?"

"BOFF!" squealed Charlotte. "*You don't mean. . .!!*"

Boff nodded.

"I do mean. I actually believe there must be *two more beams* marked with pirates. . ."

CHAPTER THIRTEEN

Arah-song

Mr Leonard opened his front door and stepped back in surprise. The five Naitabals stood on his doorstep, each of them carrying a small bag, with Ben and Charlotte carrying bigger ones.

"This is an unexpected pleasure," said Mr Leonard. "Come in, come in."

He turned to let them pass, and they went again into the little sitting-room where they had had their first meeting.

"How's the spring-cleaning going?" said Mr Leonard, joining them. "Sit down, everyone, sit down."

"The cleaning's going fine," said Boff. Then, when everyone was settled, he pulled something out of his own small bag and gave it to Mr Leonard. "We really came to bring you this."

Mr Leonard looked down at the little brown paper parcel that Boff had placed in his hands.

"That's very kind of you. . ." he began. "But you don't have to bring me anything. It's me that owes you all for cleaning the house for me. You know I couldn't have done it myself, and I can't afford to have anyone doing it for me. . ."

Slowly, Mr Leonard unwrapped the brown paper. When he pulled back the edges to reveal the contents, like the Naitabals, he couldn't believe his eyes. He actually rubbed his eyes and opened them again as he stared down at the bundle of £50 notes that was sitting in his lap. He rifled through the notes.

"There must be *five thousand pounds* here," he said. "You

shouldn't be carrying this amount of money through the streets. Where on earth did you find it?"

It was the Naitabals' big moment.

"With this," said Jayne, leaning forward and placing another bundle on Mr Leonard's lap.

"And this," said Toby, doing the same.

"And this," said Charlotte.

"And this," said Ben.

Mr Leonard's eyes nearly bulged out of his head.

"Children!" he gasped. "That's. . . that's *twenty five thousand pounds*! I can't believe this is happening! Where did you get it?"

"Are you ready for an even bigger shock?" said Boff.

Mr Leonard looked up, tearing his eyes away from the mountain of money on his lap.

"You haven't. . ."

Slowly, carefully, Boff pulled a little coffee table into their midst and slowly, carefully, the Naitabals unloaded their sacks on to it. Not a word was said as the piles of £50 notes grew higher and higher and bundles started landsliding on to the carpet.

When all the sacks were empty and the coffee table was nowhere to be seen under the pile, Boff said, "We'd love to be able to use it to buy Gray's Wood, but the money's not ours. It's yours. But at least we hope it means you won't have to sell Gray's Wood after all."

Mr Leonard was still looking bewildered and had lost count of the bundles minutes ago. He looked up again as if appealing for help.

Charlotte gave him a sunny smile.

"It's three hundred thousand pounds," she said, as if she'd just counted the money in her piggy bank. "We found it hidden in the attic in Deep Shadow Cottage, so it must be yours because you own the house."

"Wh-what do you mean, you found it in the attic? You

mean you just went up into the attic and found it lying in a heap, or what?"

Slowly, between them, the Naitabals told Mr Leonard the whole story, starting with Jayne seeing the face at the window of the cottage, then their strange find in the rubbish that the foxes had strewn about. Then how they had tricked Cedric into giving up the teddy bear, and finally to their solving the rhyming clue that led them to the money – money that was so well concealed that even a team of police scientists wouldn't have found it unless they'd had the teddy bear themselves.

As he listened, Mr Leonard didn't speak a single word throughout. Even at the end he said nothing, but just looked at them with his face registering sadness.

"It means you won't have to sell Gray's Wood, now, Mr Leonard, doesn't it?" Jayne said brightly. "You said two hundred thousand would be enough to live on. Now you'll have some left over as well."

Mr Leonard shook his head, and suddenly the Naitabals realised that something was wrong.

"What's the matter, Mr Leonard?" said Charlotte. "Have we done something bad?"

Mr Leonard forced a little smile and shook his head again.

"Of course you haven't done anything bad," he said. "You've done a marvellous thing. You're all geniuses, and no mistake. I'm not sure many people could have done what you've done, but. . ." Mr Leonard's face fell.

"But what?" said Ben.

"But I can't take the money."

"What?"

"Why not?"

"What's the problem?"

"I can't take the money because it doesn't belong to me. It must belong to Sarah, whoever Sarah is. It was Sarah's teddy bear, and it's Sarah's money. Sarah's little treasure. I

131

can only guess that 'Deedy' is the man who gave me the cottage and the woods. It doesn't matter if I tell you now. His name was Derek Daniel Fern: DD Fern. I can only suppose that's where the 'Dee-dee' comes from. . ."

"Did you say *'Fern'*?" said Boff suddenly. Then, "Sorry, I didn't mean to interrupt."

"If he left that teddy bear with that message in it for Sarah, then he meant Sarah to find the money. The money is her 'little treasure' – can you see that? I can't possibly take it. It would be stealing in a big way. I know it's sad for all of us, but I'm afraid the situation's the same as it was before. I've got no money, and I have to sell the woods and the cottage to pay for my retirement. I can't see any way out of it."

"If the money was for Sarah," said Charlotte, "why didn't this Mr Fern just keep it in a savings account and leave it to her in his will?"

Mr Leonard shook his head again.

"I've no idea," he said. "He must have hidden it for a good reason, but who knows? All I know is, it doesn't make any difference to you or me."

Mr Leonard stood up.

"I'm very grateful to you all for what you're doing – cleaning the house and everything – and now finding this. I'm sorry I can't sound more grateful."

The Naitabals took the hint and stood up as Mr Leonard swept an arm across the mountain of money.

"Does anyone else know you've found this?" he said.

Boff shook his head.

"No."

"Well, there's no way I can let you walk back through the streets carrying three hundred thousand pounds in cash. . . There's also the problem of where we're going to keep it until this Sarah turns up to claim it."

"Could you pay it into your account until then?" said Charlotte. "You might as well earn some interest on it."

Mr Leonard shook his head again.

"I don't mind telling you children that I feel very nervous about this money. I'm afraid there's no way I can pay it into my account. What would my bank manager say? Hello, he'd say, here's a customer who's been earning an honest little wage for forty years, putting the money in regularly, and spending it even more regularly, and suddenly he walks in with three hundred thousand pounds in cash. What's he going to think? The first thing he'd do after paying it in would be to call the police, I shouldn't wonder. Thanks for your trust, kids, but not for me, thank you."

"I know what we can do," said Ben. He glanced at the others for approval. "If we could use Mr Leonard's telephone, we could ask Mr Elliott to come and collect us in his van. He left at the same time as us, so he should be back home by now. He'd give us a safe journey, and he'd probably know what to do next."

The other Naitabals agreed that it sounded like a good idea.

"This Mr Elliott," said Mr Leonard. "Do you trust him completely? We're talking a lot of money here."

"He's been our friend for years, Mr Leonard," said Boff. "We'd trust Mr Elliott to the ends of the earth."

Boff told Mr Leonard some of the adventures he'd been involved in, and how he was helping them clean and decorate the cottage without prying into their secrets.

Mr Leonard nodded approval and fetched the telephone, and Charlotte made the call.

"Mr Elliott? Hello, it's Charlotte. We wondered if you could do us a very special favour. There's a really good reason for it, but I can't tell you over the telephone. We wondered, would you mind collecting us from a house in the village if I give you the address?"

Charlotte nodded round at everyone, then gave Mr Elliott the address. While they waited, Boff asked another question.

"Mr Leonard, I hope you don't mind me asking, but did

133

you ever buy a house in Brunswick Road and sell it again?"

Mr Leonard nodded.

"Well, I did, and I didn't. It was Derek Fern who bought it and sold it, but he used my name because he didn't want his wife to find him. There was a terrible end to their marriage, he told me that much. He didn't want to leave any sort of trail."

"Thank you," said Boff. "So you are the Mr Leonard who owned it, but it was Deedy Fern who went there? That explains the house where we found the teddy bear, anyway."

Five minutes later, they all heard the rattling of a noisy van outside. They gathered up their sacks, said goodbye to Mr Leonard, and went out to meet Mr Elliott.

Apart from lots of thanks, the Naitabals said nothing during the journey, mostly because the noise inside Mr Elliott's van was so bad that it was almost impossible to hear anything. As soon as the van was parked and the engine stopped, the Naitabals followed Mr Elliott into his house. Mr Elliott never asked for explanations, and if the Naitabals hadn't wanted to tell him why they wanted a lift, he would have thought nothing of it. But once inside the security of Mr Elliott's house, the Naitabals drew his curtains for him, put his kettle on to boil, and tipped out the contents of their sacks on to the kitchen table.

"Coo!" said Mr Elliott. "I wish I could charge that much for decorating!"

The Naitabals laughed and then took turns to explain everything to Mr Elliott, exactly as they had explained everything to Mr Leonard. They added their fears about Gray's Wood being sold, and how Mr Leonard had refused to take the money, and how they didn't know what to do with it, and didn't know how to find the missing Sarah. When they had finished and Boff had poured cups of tea for everyone, Mr Elliott pronounced judgement.

"Well, Sarah's not a problem," he said, and laughed. "And the cash ain't a problem. Anythin' else I can do for yer, mates?"

The Naitabals looked askance at Mr Elliott, knowing he was enjoying teasing them. Mr Elliott never seemed to take anything too seriously – except when it was *very* serious. He really was their very best friend.

"What do you mean, Mr Elliott?" said Charlotte, smiling sweetly.

"I thought you might like to see this," he said, waving an envelope at them. "It's a letter that came this mornin', but I didn't open it straight off, like, seein' as I was waylaid by you lot."

He seemed to be giving the envelope to Charlotte more than anyone, so she took it carefully, glancing at the others for approval, and turned it over. It was covered in New Zealand stamps, and the address had been written in what looked like a child's handwriting.

"Thank you, Mr Elliott. Shall I read it to everyone now?"

"Might as well," said Mr Elliott. "It's not goin' to read itself, is it?"

Charlotte opened the flap of the envelope, which had already been unstuck, and extracted the letter inside.

"I've read it, now, o' course," said Mr Elliott. "But I might as well listen again, to see if I got it right."

The contents were written in the same neat handwriting as the address.

"*Dear Mr Elliott,*" Charlotte began to read, "*I don't know if you remember me, but I'm writing to ask for your help. About seven years ago, when I was six years old (I'm thirteen now), I came to spend a few days with my cousin in the house next door to yours. My mother was ill in hospital and my father thought it would be best if I went to stay with my aunt and uncle. I'll always remember my holiday there. I met other children in the street who were really nice, a*

135

little girl called Charlotte who was only three –" Charlotte flushed and broke off – "She doesn't mean *me*, does she?" – then continued reading, "*I remember Charlotte and my cousin and me sitting on Charlotte's kitchen table with a pair of scales, weighing everything we could find and making strange pies that tasted horrible.*" Charlotte broke off again. "I remember that!"

"*I helped to dry the dishes, too,*" Charlotte read on, "*and cut my finger on the bread knife. There was another boy of five called Barry. He wore round glasses and used to ride on the back of his big Alsatian dog.*"

All eyes turned to Boff. It was a long time since he'd been the little Barry Offord with round glasses. He grinned.

"I did use to do that, yes," he admitted.

"*You might remember,*" Charlotte continued, "*that you gave us all a ride in your van, Mr Elliott, and helped us climb some trees in the woods opposite. My mother tells me that you've lived in your house all your life, so that's why I'm writing to your address, because there's a good chance you'll still be there. I know that my cousin moved from her house next door soon after. I can't remember anyone else's surname, so I don't know if they still live there. I thought it would be safest to write to you. I hope you can help.*

"*When I came to stay, I brought my teddy bear with me. I loved my Teddy, especially as he had been given to me by my Uncle Deedy (his name was Derek D Fern, but he liked being called Uncle Deedy). It was Uncle Deedy who took us to the house to stay with his brother's children (my cousins). During the stay my Teddy disappeared, and my cousin Felicity said she'd hidden it, and wouldn't give it back. When I told my aunt she just laughed and said Felicity would give it back before I went home. Well, Felicity didn't give it back. I was heartbroken. Felicity had gone to a dancing lesson when Uncle Deedy came to collect me, and no one could find Teddy, so I had to go, and Aunt Peggy said she'd*

136

find it and send it back. Well, she never did. Only a few months later they moved to the north of England and my family emigrated to New Zealand."

"It's a long letter," said Jayne.

"There's not much more," said Ben, looking over Charlotte's shoulder.

"*About a year ago*," Charlotte read on, "*I made contact with my cousin again, and she said she was very sorry about my Teddy, and how selfish and horrible she must have been to hide it. But she said it was a very good, very secret hiding place, so good that she thought there was every chance Teddy would still be there. She sent me a diagram of where her secret hiding place was. I would have loved to get my Teddy back, but of course I didn't do anything about it. I felt too embarrassed to write to strangers who would be living in that house now. But then something else happened. Sadly, a few days ago, my Uncle Deedy died. He has sent news that Teddy is keeping a secret for me (whatever that means!). That's what has made me pluck up the courage to write. Now that Uncle's gone, I'd love to have Teddy (and his little secret) as a memento.*

"*If you can help me find my long-lost Teddy, I'd be most grateful. I enclose enough International Postal Coupons to pay for him to be sent home to me by airmail if you find him. If you don't, or can't help, please use the enclosed addressed envelope to tell me what's happened, or put me in touch with the people who live in that house now.*

"*Thank you for reading this very long letter, with love and hoping for good news, yours very sincerely,*

"*Sarah Padbury."*

Charlotte looked up and grinned.

"Coo!" said Mr Elliott. "You lot don't hang about, do yer? The letter only came this mornin', and you've done it already! Before you even looked at it! Found the little secret, and all!"

"Shall I read the letter to Sarah from her Uncle Deedy, as well?" said Charlotte.

"Might as well," said Mr Elliott. "It adds a bit more to the picture."

Charlotte read:

"Dearest Sarah,

"This letter (sent to you by my solicitor) brings with it the news that my life has come to an end. I'm sorry that there's so little for you. I would have left you everything I owned if it hadn't been for the evil Josie Fern – the woman I stupidly married. I was old and gullible and she was young and greedy. She only wanted me so she could get her poisonous talons into my bank account. As you already know, I had to get rid of everything to prevent her getting her nasty claws into any of my money. However, I have managed to hide a little treasure for you – it's our little secret. No one reading this letter will know where the gift is hidden, because only you will know the answer. Do you remember where you lost your favourite teddy bear? Of course you do. Well, I found him. I hope he's still there – plan enclosed. Now only he knows where your gift can be found. It's worth travelling to England, I assure you. Find him, solve the clue, and you will find what I managed to keep for you. Don't let the wicked Josie Fern get it!

"Have a long and happy life and think of me kindly sometimes.

"Your ever-loving,

"Uncle Deedy."

Charlotte stopped reading.

"So that's why he gave the woods away," said Ben. "So Mrs Fern couldn't get them."

"And look," said Charlotte, "Here's the *real* drawing of Cedric's bedroom with the cross and 'Teddy Bear Hidden Here'."

"It seems funny it's been all the way to New Zealand and

back already," said Toby.

"He wrote to her because he knew he was dying," said Boff, looking sad. "It must have been Uncle Deedy's face you saw at the window, Jayne. He must have cycled to the hospital later that day, and posted the letter to New Zealand on the way. . ."

"And that's why Sarah has written to Mr Elliott," said Charlotte. "Because her uncle died."

"It all happened because Deedy died. . ." murmured Boff.

"Well, that's it, then," said Mr Elliott, after a pause. He winked at them all, gave a little half smile, and suddenly turned and reached on to the kitchen dresser for his cheque book. "I'll just write her a cheque, and I can send it with the teddy bear. That'll give her a nice surprise!"

"*A nice surprise. . .!*" squealed Jayne, as she saw Mr Elliott writing a cheque for three hundred thousand pounds.

"Well, it won't bounce," said Mr Elliott, waving a hand across the table. "I'll pay this cash in tomorrer, so that's no problem."

"Won't. . . won't your bank manager say something?" said Jayne, remembering what Mr Leonard had said. "Won't he. . . won't he call the police?"

"Coo! He'll lose my account if he does," said Mr Elliott. "I've had an account there for forty-five years. Longer than the manager's been alive. Must have paid 'em a fortune by now, so a bit more won't make no difference."

He finished writing the cheque and showed it to them.

"There you are. I'll write Sarah a little note to go with it."

"Thank you, Mr Elliott!"

Charlotte and the others gazed at the cheque, awestruck.

Mr Elliott had solved the problem of getting the money to Sarah, but there were still some unanswered questions nagging at the Naitabals. Mrs Fern was one of them, still waiting for a teddy bear. And there were still a few mysteries about her ex-husband.

They all started thinking about their next move as Mr Elliott disappeared upstairs to the bathroom, but Ben was the first one to speak.

"What I still don't understand," he said, "is why on earth Mr Fern was making photocopies of £50 notes when he had three hundred thousand pounds in the attic?"

"Perhaps," said Charlotte, "he wanted Sarah to have every single penny, and he didn't want to spend any himself. Perhaps he only copied a few to keep himself going."

"But he must have copied hundreds!" said Jayne. "The plates were all set up for *mass production*!"

"And they wouldn't have fooled anybody," said Ben. "No one would be fooled by colour photocopies, not close up."

"He obviously stopped Mrs Fern getting any money," said Boff, "but if she married him for his money, how did he convince her that he had none left?"

"Never mind all that," said Toby slowly, "how are we going to save Gray's Wood from the builders? That's what I want to know.

In the excitement, the others had almost forgotten their biggest problem of all. Mr Leonard still had no money, so the situation was exactly the same as before.

"And where's the other half of the piece of paper that Mr Leonard showed us?" said Jayne. "The one he needs before he can sell?"

Ben's face suddenly lit up as he grinned at each of his friends in turn.

"I've just had an idea," he said, looking pleased with himself. "I think I know how we can do a couple of things. Put Mrs Fern off the scent, and get our own back on the Igmopong for telling her about the teddy bear." He leaned forward and started explaining his ideas just as Mr Elliott came back into the kitchen.

"Coo!" he said. "Can I join in? I'd love to see her face when she finds out!"

140

CHAPTER FOURTEEN

Midnight Beasts

On Friday morning, Naitabal Territory was filled with strange and secret activities.

In the local town, two girls were scouring the shops for a teddy bear, but not just any teddy bear. It had to be less than thirty centimetres tall, dark brown, with brown glass-button eyes and a red ribbon round its neck.

In a cottage deep in the woods, two boys, one with glasses, watched in dim light as a machine whirred in front of them, back and forth, back and forth. Their eyes shone with excitement as their faces flickered bright and dark, rhythmically with the flashing of a light, on and off, on and off.

In a tree-house, a boy was drawing a map. At the top he was writing the initials 'G.W.', trying to imitate someone else's handwriting. Towards the right was a little house marked 'D.S.C.', and towards the left were two oak trees with an 'X' marked between them. A dotted line, marked '200m' ran from the house westwards to the 'X'.

Some time later, two girls stepped down from a bus. Before the bus drove away, they placed a brand new dark brown teddy bear in front of its back wheel. The bus moved off and flattened the teddy bear. The girls laughed and picked it up, rubbed it in the dust, then dragged it all the way home on the end of a piece of string. When they reached home, they cut it open, pushed things inside it and stitched it up again.

An hour later, between two oak trees in the woods, five children were taking it in turns to dig a deep hole, two digging, three on watch.

No one saw them.

An hour after that, two girls delivered a chest to a lady at the hotel where she was staying. The chest had metal straps like a pirate's treasure chest, and fifteen pirate figures branded into the lid, along with the legend, 'SARAH'S LITTLE TREASURE'. Inside the chest was a very worn, rather dirty, dark brown teddy bear.

It was Friday afternoon, and the day of the Igmopong's midnight feast was already halfway through. Cedric had spent part of the morning, goggle-eyed, watching his mother's preparations for the hampers. There were jellies and blancmanges, cream doughnuts, jam doughnuts, meringues, cream slices, custard slices, six flavours of fizzy drinks, and crisps and savouries and surprise party packs. His mother had made lovely little iced cakes, specially decorated with Cedric's and Doris's and their friends' initials on the top of each one. He picked up one of the ones with 'CM' on it and ate it while his mother was out of the kitchen for three seconds. It was delicious, and his face glowed at the thought of approaching midnight.

Outside, Cedric saw the Naitabals over his garden fence. Much as he was bursting to crow about his secret, to his credit he bottled it up, and gave no clue to the forthcoming clandestine event. He had had too many treats wrecked by the Naitabals in the past (always because of something he'd done to them) to take chances.

"Hello Ben, hello Charlotte. Hello Barry, hello Jayne, hello Toby," he said.

The Naitabals gave no hint that they knew his secret, either. They had learned the supreme advantage of surprise. They greeted him politely in return. It was a little scene that would have filled Mrs Morgan's heart with joy, and hope for an end to their silly life-long feud.

"I suppose you're completely better now?" said Charlotte.

"Yes, thank you," said Cedric.

"Good. We can't catch any germs off you, then."

The polite interlude had passed.

Mrs Fern answered the telephone in her bedroom, then came down to the reception area of the small hotel where she was staying, to find two young girls waiting for her. The taller one, who had fair hair in a pony tail, handed her a carrier bag containing a wooden box.

"Your teddy bear," she said.

Mrs Fern grabbed the package without saying thank you. She glanced in the bag and read the words burned on to the box, 'SARAH'S LITTLE TREASURE'. She seemed grumpily satisfied.

"Is this everything?" she demanded.

"Yes." Both girls answered at once.

"Goodbye, then."

Mrs Fern turned and went back to her room.

With the door shut, she took the box from the bag and opened the lid. Lying inside was a scruffy teddy bear that just fitted the box. She pulled it out, turned it over, and saw the note on its back, written in her ex-husband's scrawl, 'With love from Deedy'. Mrs Fern breathed a sigh of satisfaction. At least they had given her the right teddy bear.

She took off the note, then started feeling the bear just as Charlotte had done a few days before, pressing its head, limbs and stomach in turn. It was when she pressed the stomach that she felt the tell-tale rustle of paper. She reached for her handbag, rummaged for her nail scissors, then carefully slit open the stitches in the seam down its back. She wrenched open the wound and plunged her greedy long-nailed fingers into its interior. Her face lit up in triumph as she found a small sheet of paper folded in four.

"Got you!" exclaimed Mrs Fern. She unfolded the little

package, and her eyes bulged with greed as she saw that it was a map. At the top were the initials 'G.W.', and the map looked like this:

It didn't name anything on the map, but to anyone who knew, the initials at the top meant Gray's Wood, and 'D.S.C.' by the little house in the trees meant Deep Shadow Cottage. A dotted line ran in a westward direction from the cottage, with '200m' marked against it, ending at a pair of oak trees and a cross. It was a simple map, and needed no great brain to solve its directions. All Josie Fern had to do was to pace two hundred metres west from the cottage, find the two oak trees, and dig.

She could hardly contain her excitement. She immediately jumped into her car and drove to Deep Shadow Cottage. It was deserted. She no longer had the key, but it didn't matter now. She walked quickly to the west side, then glanced down at her feet and back to the cottage.

"About five metres," she murmured under her breath. Then, counting aloud, she started walking to the west. "Six, seven, eight. . ."

As she approached the count of two hundred, she could see ahead of her two mature oak trees, quite close together. There were no other oak trees close by, so she knew that these must be the pair on the map. She was in a part of the wood now with no paths nearby, and consequently quite secluded – but not secluded enough to go digging in the hours of daylight. That was far too risky.

When was the best time? Ten o'clock? Eleven? Twelve? She decided on twelve, when even the most enthusiastic night walkers would be back home having cups of cocoa. Yes, twelve would be much safer.

She needed a spade and a lamp. She would go and buy them now. Then, at twelve o'clock, she would come back into Gray's Wood and find Sarah's Little Treasure.

The Naitabals' parents had given them all permission to sleep in the Naitabal tree-house, but by eleven o'clock that evening, it was deserted.

At that time, the Naitabals were crouched behind bushes in Gray's Wood, not far from Deep Shadow Cottage. Ben, keeping his voice to a whisper, reminded them once more of what they had to do.

At five minutes past eleven the first of the Igmopong parents arrived at Deep Shadow Cottage. It was easy to find, because the lamps at each corner were already burning brightly, placed there by Colonel Slack twenty minutes before. At exactly ten past eleven, a small herd of parents penetrated the darkness with their torches, carrying strips of white linen. They were followed in the rear by the hamper-bearers. The sharp undertones of Colonel Slack could be heard as he led the way, barking out his orders from the master plan, marking the trees with the white linen bandages.

With military precision they reappeared at the cottage at twenty minutes to twelve, then scattered to take up their guard duties at the entrances to the wood.

As soon as the sound of Colonel Slack's high-pitched but commanding voice was heard retreating from the woods, the Naitabals crept silently from their hiding place. They were familiar with every tree and bush in the woods, even in the dark. They carried out their next task with an efficiency that might have won Colonel Slack's grudging admiration, had he ever found out about it.

At a quarter to twelve precisely Mr Morgan arrived at Deep Shadow Cottage with the four Igmopong and three friends, who were all in a state of hungry excitement.

"Now these are the rules," Mr Morgan repeated in a listless voice. "We don't want you getting lost in these woods in the middle of the night, so we've tied white linen to every third tree to show you the way to the feast. Just follow the trail and you can't go wrong."

The Igmopong's faces glowed with excitement as they met Colonel Slack, who filled in the rest of the rules.

"Eventually you'll come to a small circle of white tree markers – quite unmistakable – and it's in that circle that the hampers are hidden – under a couple of bushes – nothing too difficult. Enjoy your feast. When you've finished, just stay where you are, shout nice and loud, and we'll come in and join you to pick up the hampers and lead you out. Understood?"

The Igmopong understood.

"And if there's any trouble at all, or any problem, just shout and we'll be there in a few minutes."

Cedric and his friends nodded.

"And whatever else you do, *don't leave the trail*."

The Igmopong promised they wouldn't leave the trail.

Mr Morgan gave Cedric a torch, and the Igmopong set off along the trail to their midnight feast. There was very little moonlight, and they were soon out of sight of the lamps surrounding the cottage. The small torch gave little comfort to a group of children who in daylight were mostly frightened of cows. Cedric flashed the torch ahead of them looking for blazes of white on the trunks of trees.

"There's the first one!" he shouted.

"There's another!" squeaked Amanda.

The trail of white linen led them deeper and deeper into the woods – much deeper than Cedric had anticipated. Each new sighting was therefore greeted with glee, and their faces soon began to glow with the exercise. The only thing that kept at bay their abject fear of darkness was the thought that they would soon be doing what they all enjoyed most of all – eating.

The trail led on and on and they clung to the back of each other's clothes, more for comfort than for guidance.

"Do you think we're nearly there?" said Martin, nervously.

"We'd better be," said Doris. "My legs are getting tired."

Cedric gained courage from the sight of another friendly white tag.

"Huh! The stupid old Naitabals'll be mad when we tell them about this in the morning," he said, puffing. "It's a jolly good idea of mine, isn't it?"

"Ours!" said Doris belligerently. "It was *our* idea, not yours!"

"All right, then, ours. And no silly Naitabals to come and spoil anything."

They all agreed it was a good idea, and they all hoped they'd soon be there. They walked on, quickening their pace slightly.

"And even if the stupid Naitabals did come, all we've got to do is shout for our parents, and they'd come right away, wouldn't they?"

They all agreed that they would.

"But the Naitabals are all in bed!" gloated Cedric. "Those silly softie Naitabals all tucked up in bed, and we're out here hunting through the deep woods in the dead of night! Hee, hee! Softie old Ben and Charlotte and the others!"

"Oy," said Doris suddenly. She had taken over the lead and had stopped in front with the torch.

"Are we there?" said Cedric. There was gleeful anticipation and relief in his voice.

147

"No. But we passed this tree before. Look – it's the one with the initials carved in it."

"No – it's a different one. Let's get on, I'm starving."

They got on.

Next time it was Cedric who stopped with the torch. He was panting hard, and a note of impatience had crept into his voice.

"Where's the stupid circle, that's what I want to know?"

"Perhaps we've missed it," said Freddie.

"They said we *couldn't* miss it," said Doris, annoyed.

"Let's go back and see," volunteered Leila.

"It's no use going *back*, let's get *on*," said Cedric, feeling his stomach rumbling.

"We must be nearly there by now," said Martin.

Again they went on, but this time their pace had slackened. Privately, Cedric was beginning to think it was a rotten idea after all, and that he'd have enjoyed a feast much more in the warmth and comfort of one of their bedrooms. He started to voice his opinion that the fathers had made the trail too long and tiring. His mood was not improved when Doris stopped them for the third time.

"There's that tree again," she said, pointing.

The torch was now a dim yellow colour and was beginning to flicker. They all stood and looked at the initials – unmistakably the same initials – that were carved on the same – unmistakable – tree.

Suddenly they heard a noise.

"What's that?" said Andy.

"It sounded like someone digging," said Doris.

"Can't be," said Amanda. "Not at this time of night."

Cedric stamped his foot.

"I'm hungry! I haven't eaten anything since tea *specially* for this, and the sides of my stomach are sticking together! There must be a rotten circle here somewhere. It's all your stupid fathers have done this," he added, turning on Martin,

Leila and Freddie. "They've organised it wrong, and I'm fed up."

"It was your rotten idea," retorted Freddie. "Rather a stupid one, if you ask me."

"Oh, yes, and you all agreed it was a good idea until your rotten fathers messed it up."

"What's the use arguing," said Amanda. "We've been past this tree three times, which must mean we've missed a turning somewhere."

Just then an owl screeched above them and turned their already chilled blood to ice.

"Maybe we'll see the trail easier if we go the other way," suggested Martin, nervously.

They went the other way, clinging to each other in a group rather than a straight line. And when they had returned to the same tree for the fourth time, Cedric felt like crying. He was hot and tired and hungry and he was furious with everyone and everything.

"They've spoilt it!" he stamped. "They've messed it all up. I'm fed up, and it's your fathers' faults and I'm *starving*."

"I think we should call for help," said Andy. It was the only sensible thing he'd said all day.

They called for help.

At the time when Cedric and the Igmopong were setting off from the entrance to the woods in Brunswick Road, Mrs Josie Fern was thrusting her new spade into the soft earth between the twin oak trees.

She had been alarmed to see the bright lights surrounding the cottage, and disturbed when she first heard the distant voices. Her first thought had been a worry that someone else was after the same treasure. But no one was very close, and she paced the two hundred long steps, starting in the bright lanterns that marked the corners of the cottage. As she moved further into the shadows of the midnight wood, she realised with relief that she was in her part of it alone.

The earth was softer than she had imagined, and the digging went well. She was only thirty centimetres down when the spade struck something. At the same moment she heard children's voices in the middle distance. She dimmed her lamp to a tiny glow and looked up, peering through the trees. She could have sworn that she saw a torch flickering through the dark trees some distance away. The voices receded, and Mrs Fern, very excited now, dug out a few more spadefuls of earth, then stooped down to see what she had found. At the same moment, the children's voices approached again. She switched off her lamp altogether and waited until the voices, now arguing, faded again into the darkness along with their flickering light.

This was her chance. She switched on her lamp again and tugged at the bag that her spade had exposed. It came out easily. It was a huge clear plastic sack, and she felt a thrill of ecstasy run through her as her lamp lit up the contents. Through the transparent sides of the sack, she could see bundles of £50 notes, each bundle secured with brown paper bands. And there were scores of them. She quickly calculated that she must be looking at fifty thousand, perhaps as much as a hundred thousand pounds.

She breathed heavily in deep happiness and excitement and exclaimed "Yes!" under her breath. As she stood up to go, she heard the children approaching for the third time. This time they were definitely whining.

Horrible children. She hoped they were lost.

She reached her car, after making a wide berth round a man who seemed to be guarding an entrance to the wood, opened the boot, tossed the plastic sack inside and slammed down the lid. In the almost total darkness she could see very little, but she heard the dull crackly thud of the boot shutting. It didn't sound right. It hadn't closed cleanly. She tugged it but it wouldn't open. She probed for the keyhole with her key and felt the corner of the plastic bag sticking out underneath the lock. She turned the key to free it, but it refused to turn. She was afraid of using more force in case she broke the key. The corner of the bag had jammed the mechanism.

She muttered a rude word under her breath, then drove the car slowly back to her hotel.

In the hotel car park, Mrs Josie Fern looked at her watch. One-thirty. She couldn't call someone out at this time of night to open a car boot. Anyway, what would such a stranger think of a late night call to unlock a bag of money? He might even run off with it. Worse, she didn't dare leave the car on its own in the car park for the rest of the night. What if someone stole it?

Mrs Josie Fern said another rude word, locked herself in the car, and settled down for what would be a long, long night without a wink of sleep.

The Naitabals sat in a circle in a remote part of the wood. In the middle of the Naitabal circle was a large hamper, and from this with satisfying regularity one Naitabal hand or another would extract a cake, a cream doughnut or a meringue and transfer it with unerring accuracy, in the dark, to the owner's mouth. This activity was not accompanied by conversation for several reasons. The first was that it was imperative that they made as little sound as possible for fear of being overheard by the Igmopong or their fathers. The second was that at the rate their mouths were consuming the contents of the hamper it was physically impossible to combine both speech and mastication. The third was they were all in such a dream-like trance of pleasure that the manifestation of speech was unnecessary.

The plan had been satisfyingly simple. By untying some white linen markers and retying them strategically elsewhere, they had created a path that had led their victims to a different part of the wood, and eventually into a long circular path. As soon as the Igmopong were in it, the Naitabals had deftly removed the markers that led to it, leaving their sworn enemies to circle endlessly with no means of finding their way out again.

By the time they heard the first distant cries for help, the Naitabals had finished the first hamper, and were stuffing the last few cakes into their pockets.

"Let's go!" hissed Ben.

They replaced the empty hamper where they had found it with its partner under some bushes, then began to make their way out of the wood. They chose the opposite direction from the distant, but perceptibly growing, commotion. As they made their stealthy escape, the frightened cries of the lost Igmopong echoed through the darkened woods. The sounds mingled satisfyingly with the answering shouts of lost parents. . .

The Naitabals, always thorough, returned to the woods before breakfast the following morning and returned the trail to its original route. They then carried the hampers fifty metres to the magnetic north. Their next step was to visit the site two hundred metres west of the cottage, between the two oak trees. They discovered that a large hole had been dug there, and that its contents were missing.

Later that morning, several of the fathers retraced the trail in an attempt to solve the mystery of how the Igmopong had failed to find the feast. Standing in the original circle, and unable to find the hampers themselves, the fathers scratched their heads.

"I bet the little devils found it and ate it, and pretended they hadn't," said one.

"And they've hidden the hampers to finish off during the day," said another.

"It was funny that we couldn't find the trail when we heard them calling," said a third.

The fourth one shrugged.

"They probably untied some of the white markers to confuse us," he said, laughing. "Little scamps!"

Satisfied with this explanation, the fathers proceeded to clear the woods of their litter, and wasted no further thought on the mystery.

That afternoon, the memory of the previous dreadful night was still festering like a deep wound in Cedric Morgan's mind. His only consolation was that the Naitabals knew nothing about the humiliating failure of his cherished midnight feast.

Seeing a flash of Naitabal hovering in Mr Elliott's garden, Cedric wandered towards the fence. Hurling a few insults at a Naitabal would make him feel much better.

"Well!" he shouted, "Who had to give back the teddy bear after trying to *steal* it! Who—"

But Cedric had stopped with his mouth wide open. It wasn't a Naitabal standing in Mr Elliott's garden, but Margery. He should have known from the bright red dress that it was Margery. Seeing his approach, she had drawn from her pocket a supply of small iced cakes with Cedric's initials 'CM' iced on the top.

"Wh – wh – where did you get those?" stammered Cedric.

"It was ever so funny," said Margery, laughing and sharing the joke with him. "Last night I was lying in bed and *just before midnight* I had a really strong urge that Charlotte was in the woods with two baskets of food! Can you believe it? And I thought, well, if I'm Charlotte's *identical twin* I should have the *same powers*, shouldn't I? So I wondered if *my* powers were strong enough to move them to the north, *away from Charlotte*. So I gave it all my concentration, and guess what – I think it worked! And you'll never guess – I went

153

into the woods this morning and found them! Two huge hampers full of the loveliest things!"

She took a huge bite out of the cake with Cedric's initials on it, and smiled.

"It's amazing, isn't it?" she said, through her mouthful. "Of course, Charlotte pretended she knew nothing about it, but the 'CM' proves it, doesn't it? 'CM' *must* stand for Charlotte Maddison, mustn't it?"

Cedric was speechless.

CHAPTER FIFTEEN

End-eng

Any normal person, finding a large bag of money buried in the woods, would naturally take it straight home, look at it, feel it, count it, and possibly throw it up in the air and let it flutter down on them while they giggled hysterically.

Mrs Josie Fern, in that sense at least, was a normal person. However, although she had been looking forward to taking the big bag of money back to her hotel room, looking at it, feeling it, and counting it, the simple accident with her boot lock had prevented her from doing it. Throwing it up in the air and letting it flutter down on her while she giggled hysterically was also now impossible.

Instead, she was stirring at nine o'clock in the discomfort of her car in the hotel car park. She had had an entire sleepless night to decide that her safest course of action was to drive straight to the security of a bank.

She parked on the double yellow lines outside the front door and was inside the bank as soon as it opened, demanding a security guard to guard her car and a mechanic to open the boot lock. This already caused a stir in the bank, and all heads turned again as she strode back inside with the security guard carrying a large transparent plastic bag with £50 notes pressed to the sides like faces peering out of a frosty window.

"I want to pay that in to my account," she barked at the counter clerk. "I bank at another branch, but here's my paying-in book."

"How much is there?" said the clerk. "You haven't filled in the amount."

The combination of over-excitement, worry and absence of sleep had made Mrs Fern as snappy as a crocodile.

"I haven't the faintest idea," she screeched. "I haven't counted it. That's your job, isn't it?"

The counter clerk looked at Mrs Fern as if she were a wasp on an ice cream, then took the big bag in via the security door. Back at his position, he opened it and tipped the bundles on to his desk.

He examined the first bundle, then the next, then the next, finally looking up sharply at Mrs Fern, who was waiting impatiently, tapping her long finger-nails on the counter.

"Is this some kind of joke?" said the clerk.

"What do you mean?" snapped Mrs Fern.

"Sorry. Let me just check the rest."

"So I should think. You're there to count it, not pass comments."

The clerk finished looking at the bundles and flicking through them, then looked up at Mrs Fern.

"I'm sorry," he said. "I don't know what kind of a joke this is, but all these £50 notes are just double-sided colour photocopies."

All heads in the bank, the clerks, the customers, and the back office staff, turned to look at Mrs Fern.

Mrs Fern turned a bright crimson and looked furious.

"What do you mean. . .! There's lots of money there! There's a hundred thousand or more, there's. . ."

The clerk was holding one of the notes up to the light to show there was no mistake. There was no watermark and no metal strip. He handed one back to Mrs Fern.

"Apart from that," said the clerk, "the paper is too thin, and there seem to be only six different numbers on all the notes."

"Aren't there. . . aren't there *any* real ones?" screamed Mrs Fern.

The clerk shook his head.

Mrs Fern suddenly became aware of the absolute silence in

the bank, and everyone's attention turned towards her. In a fury, she shouted at them.

"Get on with your work, you stupid lot! Don't you know a JOKE when you see one!"

And then, with tears of humiliation flooding down her face and washing away what was left of her make-up, Mrs Fern ran from the bank.

A traffic warden was booking her car.

The Naitabals had only been back in the Naitabal tree-house for a few minutes when they saw Mr Elliott picking his way through the Sea of Debris with his quick little steps.

They invited him inside, and he climbed the rope ladder like a monkey, then settled down with them on the floor.

"I thought you might like to see these, mates," he said.

"What are they?"

"Just a letter, and a piece o' paper. Found 'em at the bank when they were counting the money in the manager's office. Tucked into one of the bundles. No way I was standing out the front there splashing three hundred thousand smackers on the counter. Not like the woman in front o' me who tried to pay in a hundred thousand in photocopies. Can't imagine where she got those, can you?" he added, with a wink.

The Naitabals and Mr Elliott all laughed, enjoying the joke.

This time Mr Elliott chose Ben to read the letter. He handed it over and Ben cleared his throat and read:

My Darling Sarah,

Now that you have found your little treasure, I'm writing to tell you the true story of your inheritance, because the last thing I want to leave behind is a mystery. You may think some of the things I've done are very mysterious or odd, but they're not really.

As you know, I used to be a fairly wealthy man. I built up

a very successful carpentry business over most of my working life, and eventually sold it for over a million pounds. I was sixty-five, I owned a lovely house, and I had all the money I needed to last me the rest of my life. I never had a wife, or children, partly because I spent all my time on the business, and probably wouldn't have made a very good husband as a result. When I died I planned to leave half to a man who saved my life, and half to you, my favourite niece. But Fate had different plans.

Soon after I retired I met a beautiful young woman who was forty years younger than me. She was so charming and wonderful, I couldn't understand what she saw in an old man like me. Having been 'swept off my feet', as they say, I was too stupid to realise that what she saw in me wasn't a handsome, mature man – but an old fogey with a million quid!

We married within a few months, and our first few weeks together seemed like heaven. But very quickly she changed character. The sweet smile camouflaged a wicked heart. Her smiling lips turned down the other way and took on a habit of criticism. Her shining eyes narrowed to a look of hatred – as if I had done anything to make her hate me!

By this time she was throwing my money around like garden compost, and making the rest of my life hell. Within a few months she was demanding a divorce – and half my money!

I'm afraid the law is rather stupid like that – it says that a few months of happiness – followed by several months of hell – were going to cost me half of what I'd worked for for over forty years!

I realised too late that there was no fool like an old fool like me, and felt relieved that at least she hadn't poisoned me and got *all* my money.

Quite honestly, losing half my money wouldn't have made any difference to the quality of my life – I would still have a nice house and everything I needed. But it was the principle of the thing. This woman had never loved me the slightest bit – she was just acting very convincingly that she loved me, and all the time she was planning to get rid of me and get her claws into a nice easy million pounds!

For that reason I determined that she wouldn't get a penny. I had to act quickly.

Some of the things I did, you may not fully understand, but you will learn their meaning as you get older.

First, I calculated that the *land* my house stood on was worth about a hundred thousand pounds, so I took out a mortgage for that amount and handed over the deeds of the house as collateral. I then drew out all my money in cash and bought a place called Gray's Wood that had been up for sale opposite your Aunt Peggy's place. I'd noticed it was for sale on a visit there. It had something that especially interested me – a cottage in the middle of the wood that was unoccupied.

Many years before, a man had saved my life. I had been skating – rather foolishly – on the frozen river that cuts the wood in two. I fell through the ice. I was dragged by the current under the ice before I had time to grab hold of anything, but by a miracle, a man called Terry Leonard smashed the ice further downstream, hauled me out in the nick of time, and raised the alarm. I always felt grateful to Mr Leonard, but he refused to take any money as a thank you. I now felt strongly that he would be a more deserving recipient for half of my money than my scheming wife.

I bought the woods for cash in Mr Leonard's name and made them and the cottage an outright gift. I trusted Mr Leonard and gave him one unofficial condition: that I could live in the cottage for the rest of my life. Above all, he was to keep my identity a secret – no one was to know who sometimes stayed at the cottage – and no one was to know the identity of his benefactor.

I also bought your Aunt Peggy's house across the road, Sarah – the one you stayed at, and the one where you lost your teddy, of course. I had to hide the clues for you where no one else could possibly find them – and *only you* knew where you had lost your teddy. *If anyone found your teddy, they wouldn't know that 'my nest' was the house in the woods.* By the same token, if anyone searched Deep Shadow Cottage, *they would never know about your teddy, so would never find the clue to the hiding place.* Once I had attached my clues to your Teddy in Aunt Peggy's house, I had no further use for the house. I sold it again to some people called Morgan.

That was the first part of my estate dealt with.

Now I come to my wife's part.

I had already cancelled my life assurance. This meant that if I died, my wife would not get any money that way. I had also cancelled the insurance on my house and its contents. This meant that if my house was destroyed, she would not get any insurance money to replace it.

Next, I made frequent visits to Deep Shadow Cottage to finalise my plans.

The trap was set.

One evening Josie left our house to spend an evening with some of her friends, and I was then able to prepare my surprise for her return. I turned off the electricity at the mains to avoid any accidents, then went to each room of the house and sprinkled half a can of petrol across each carpet.

I then prepared a bonfire in the back garden – a bonfire of money. Most of it was in £50 notes, tied up in bundles of fifty, which meant that by the time I had drawn all the money I had left, it still amounted to two hundred bundles of £2500 each. Half a million made a nice pile, I can tell you. There was no wind, so I split a few bundles and sprinkled the individual notes over the top, along with some tens and twenties, just for luck.

My scheming wife arrived home and drove round the back of the house to the garage, where I was waiting. As she stepped out of the car, I told her I had a surprise for her. I led her into the back garden, where she saw the bonfire I had made, and while she was asking what it was all about, and why there was a stench of petrol, I threw a lighted match on the petrol trail I had laid. Three paths of flame galloped away from us, one towards the house, one to the garage, and one to the bonfire. There was a huge 'woomph!' as the garage exploded in flames, then another, bigger 'woomph!' as the house followed suit.

My wife screamed.

She screamed even more when she realised what was on the bonfire. I'd kept a bundle back to show her. She tried to grab it as I flicked through the £50 notes, but I tossed it into the flames before she could reach it. Any hope she might have had of rescuing bundles of money were gone in those first few seconds. The bonfire, also laced with petrol, erupted like a volcano. Some of the loose notes were blown away with the force of the blast, a few of them landed at her feet. And while my scheming wife screamed and ran around picking them up and stuffing them into her dress, I was hurrying around in front of her, shielding my eyes from the flames, screwing up as many notes as I could and consigning them to the fire. I don't think she collected more than a few hundred pounds.

As a last little gesture I presented her with my bank book, showing the withdrawal of £800,000 in cash over the previous few weeks.

While she was still preoccupied with more screaming and treasure grabbing, I collected the bicycle I had hidden in the bushes at a safe distance, then cycled the many miles to Deep Shadow Cottage.

The last view I had of greedy Josie was of her black silhouette against the orange flames of the house, shielding her face from the bonfire as she bent down to rescue a banknote...

We conducted our final necessary correspondence through our solicitors. I understand that she was mortified when she discovered that nothing was insured. She was even more mortified when she discovered that the hundred thousand pounds' worth of land on which the house had stood was worthless – it had to be sold to repay the hundred thousand pound loan I had so thoughtfully taken out.

So, my dearest Sarah, I was penniless. What made it all worthwhile was that my greedy Josie was penniless, too, because half of zero is zero.

But I had a little secret cottage in the woods, where I could live rent free for the rest of my life.

Does this mean that your inheritance has gone, too, Sarah? Not quite. I managed to save a little something for you. It's here.

Your loving,
Uncle Deedy.

"Wow!" said Charlotte. "That explains everything! Well, nearly everything."

"Yes," said Jayne. "Like, why did he photocopy £50 notes when he had three hundred thousand pounds in the attic?"

"This might explain it," said Mr Elliott. "This other note they found at the bank with the letter."

He reached into his overall pocket and pulled out a half sheet of blue paper.

"I went to see Mr Leonard this mornin' and he gave me this." Mr Elliott opened out the sheet, and the Naitabals recognised the list of words they had seen at Mr Leonard's house. *P.S., Don't, anyone, the, that, burnt, the, were, from, loose, nice, in, I, the, ones, you!*

Then Mr Elliott produced another sheet. It was the missing right hand sheet. On the back is said, 'You *must* take this to

Mr Leonard, the man who owns the cottage.' It was the sheet that Mr Leonard needed to allow him to sell the cottage and the woods. On the front was just another list of words: *tell, but, notes, were, on, bonfire, (apart, the, ones), photocopies, colour, kept, real, for.*

On its own, of course, it made as little sense as the left half. But then Mr Elliott held them up together, and the Naitabals were able to read the whole message:

P.S. Don't tell anyone, but the notes that were burnt on the bonfire were (apart from the loose ones) nice photocopies in colour. I kept the real ones for you!

"So *that's* why he had the copier in the basement!" said Ben.

"Come to think of it," said Charlotte, "it was covered in thick dust. Probably hadn't used it since that day."

At last everything was explained.

"And now I suppose someone's going to ask why I went to see Mr Leonard?" said Mr Elliott, looking more serious.

"No," said Jayne, turning to the others. "We weren't going to ask Mr Elliott that, were we?"

"No, Mr Elliott."

"But now you mention it. . ." said Charlotte.

Mr Elliott suddenly looked really glum.

"I might as well break it to you quick," he said. "No point in hanging around, dragging it out."

The Naitabals had never seen a gloomy look on Mr Elliott's face before, and they didn't like it.

"What, Mr Elliott?" said Charlotte.

"Well, now that Mr Leonard's seen both halves of that piece of paper, it means he can sell the cottage and the woods. I'm sorry to say he's sold it."

"What!" said Jayne.

"No!" said Toby. "As quickly as that?"

Mr Elliott nodded solemnly.

"Someone's made an offer and it's been accepted."

163

"It's horrible," said Charlotte. "It's. . . it's not a *builder*, is it?"

"I'm afraid it is," said Mr Elliott.

Charlotte buried her head in her hands.

"I want to die."

"It's the worst end to anything ever," said Boff.

"Is it really definite?" said Jayne.

"Subject to contract," said Mr Elliott, nodding his head. "But I can't see it falling through."

"There must be a chance. . ." said Toby. "Otherwise it'll be built on and we'll never be able to play there again."

"There is *some* good news, though," said Mr Elliott, brightening.

"What is it?" said Charlotte, looking up. "As if there could be any *good* news after that."

"The good news," said Mr Elliott, suddenly smirking, "is that *I'm* the builder."

There was a petrified silence.

"Well, I've been working for donkeys years, chucking me earnings into the bank, and never spending it on anything. I was in the manager's office, paying in the three hundred thousand. So I said to 'im, like, how much have I got right now, right at this second? Well, it seems I'd got loads. Some of it invested, and that's done quite nicely, and – well, to cut a long story short, *I've bought the wood*."

If ever there was a long, stunned silence in the Naitabal tree-house, it was now. None of them could have spoken if they'd tried. Boff and Ben had lumps in their throats; Toby's eyes were looking watery, although he tried to hide it; tears had sprung to Charlotte eyes, and Jayne had sprung to Mr Elliott and was hugging him.

"Coo! You'll crease my overalls doing that!" said Mr Elliott, feeling slightly embarrassed, but rather pleased. Then, when none of them answered, he couldn't resist teasing them a little bit more.

"Don't you like the idea, then?" he said. "Mr Leonard only wanted two hundred thousand for it, if he knew it would *never* be built on. So we're setting up a Naitabal Trust with him and me as trustees, so that no one can *ever* take the woods away. What do you think o' that, mates?"

"Mr Elliott, it's wonderful!" said Boff, the words coming out in little bits with catches in them.

"Mind you, I don't want a lot o' kids messing about in 'em. . ." Mr Elliott added, looking serious.

"Mr Elliott. . ."

"Only jokin', mates," he added hastily, grinning.

Then they all thanked him like he'd never been thanked before. With more kisses and hugs from the girls, and backslaps and handshakes from the boys, he made his excuses and escaped back home before he was overcome with emotion himself.

It was the best day in Naitabal history – ever.

There are now six books in
David Schutte's Naitabal Mystery series.

If you enjoyed this book, you'll love the others!

1. DANGER, KEEP OUT!
ISBN 1-904028-00-4   £5.00

Miss Coates steamed up the garden path. Her white hair glowed in the moonlight. She stopped at the well in the middle of her lawn, and shone her torch into it. And then . . . she disappeared.

To ordinary people, she's Miss Coates, but to the Naitabals she's the old enemy battleship, the SS *Coates*. And she's hiding something. Why has she grown huge hedges around her garden, so no one can see into it? And why is she so desperate to stop anyone snooping?
Determined to discover the truth, the Naitabals go investigating. But the secrets they uncover lie deep in the past – a past that Miss Coates will do anything to conceal. . .

"Get ready for an invasion of wild ten-year-olds... "

The Daily Telegraph

2. WAKE UP, IT'S MIDNIGHT!
ISBN 1-904028-01-2   £5.00

Charlotte stood, hand poised on the doorknob, and took a deep breath. The ghostly sound of typing stopped abruptly, as suddenly as it had begun. She threw open the door. A piece of paper in the old typewriter fluttered in the moving air. But there was no one there.

The Mysterious Motionless Mr Maynard hasn't moved for two days. Beneath that hairless head and ferocious scowl, his evil brain is plotting – but plotting what?
A secret drawer, an empty house at midnight, a missing manuscript, spying, cheating – and a mysterious lady in black – are just a few of the obstacles the Naitabals must overcome to solve the mystery. Wake up, it's midnight! Join the Naitabals in their second breathtaking adventure!

"The type of story that would appeal to juniors who like reading about children outwitting the adults. . . who dream of having a tree-house and outdoor adventures, and who like codes and secret letters. It is all very entertaining. . ."

Junior Bookshelf

More Naitabal Mysteries by David Schutte

3. WILD WOODS, DARK SECRET
ISBN 1-904028-02-0   £5.00

The woman was moving along a track a little way above them. Instead of walking, she seemed to be sailing effortlessly, floating like a ghost above the ground. . .

The Naitabal gang are promised the holiday of a lifetime at Mr Blake's remote country house. But from the very first moment, their visit is plunged into mystery.

Why has Mr Blake disappeared? What is the meaning of the weird coded messages? Who are the sinister strangers that prowl the dark, forbidding woods?

Only one thing is clear – Mr Blake is in big trouble. . .

"The Naitabals are a wild species of human aged about 10 who inhabit these great books. . . I hope David Schutte can keep adding to the series. . ."

The School Librarian

4. BEHIND LOCKED DOORS
ISBN 1-904028-03-9   £5.00

The message was written in purple ink on yellow paper. In an almost illegible spidery scrawl, it said...
'PLEASE HELP ME!'

Mrs Hooper has not left her home or spoken to anyone for twenty years, ever since her husband died. His hat, coat and umbrella still hang in the hall, untouched, covered in dust.

Now the Naitabals realise she might be in trouble. What sinister secrets are hidden within Mrs Hooper's spooky old house? Why has she locked herself away for so long? When the Naitabals finally open the locked doors, they find a mystery far more evil than any of them could have imagined . . .

"Have you got a Naitabal in your garden? According to author David Schutte, a Naitabal is 'a wild species of human aged about ten', it feeds on 'anything, except what its parents want it to' and it lives mainly in tree-houses. If your own Naitabal hankers for . . . adventure, buy it one of Schutte's Naitabal Mysteries."

The Times

5. GHOST ISLAND
ISBN 1-904028-05-5   £5.00

The house that was Ghost Island was silhouetted against the sky, towering above the lake. Thick, round wooden posts stuck up out of the water a few metres from it, like giant hippo teeth, encircling the whole house as far as their eyes could see.

When the Naitabals see the unusual advertisement in their local newspaper, they know they won't rest until they can unravel its strange meaning:

```
        He/she who solves this
           exquisite puzzle
     should use the digits below
         to check if it fits.
              186945
```

Its solution leads them to Ghost Island – and to a mystery that has remained unsolved for fourteen years.

It's the Naitabals' biggest challenge yet.

SKELETONS IN THE ATTIC
ISBN 1-904028-04-7   £5.00

Peter stared at Joe, unable to speak, his neck and jaw muscles paralysed and his eyes filling with tears. Joe, alarmed, picked up the diary from where it had fallen and frantically turned the pages. . .

Peter, recovering from the sudden death of his mother six weeks before, has never known his father, believing him to be dead. His horrible Uncle Len has moved in, and Peter's future is looking bleak.

Then disturbing things start happening. First, a strange man in a sports car starts watching the house and asking the neighbours questions. Then someone telephones Peter, claiming to be his father. It's only when Peter and his friend Joe start messing around in the attic that they find something so shocking that it changes Peter's life for ever. . .

(There are no Naitabals in this book, but the story sets the scene for the fifth Naitabal mystery, *Ghost Island.*)

"I enjoyed this book very much and would definitely recommend it to my friends."
Paul Bailey, aged 9

"Skeletons in the Attic is a brilliant book."

Chloe Jones, aged 10

Junior Genius